Something Blue

Something Blue

edited by
JENNA JAMESON
with
M. CATHERINE OLIVERSMITH

SOUNDS PUBLISHING™

Savannah, Georgia

Text copyright © 2008 Sounds Publishing, Inc.

Published by: Sounds Publishing, Inc.
            7400 Abercorn Street, Suite 705–300
            Savannah, GA 31406
            www.soundsmedia.com

CIP data is available.

ISBN-10: 0-9777105-9-9
ISBN-13: 978-0-9777105-9-1

Printed and manufactured in the United States of America

10 9 8 7 6 5 4 3 2 1

For additional information on **JennaTales**, *Erotica for the woman on top,* or to download audio erotica, visit www.jennatales.com.

This first collection of sexy JennaTales is devoted to all Jenna's loyal and loving fans. Especially, these stories are for the amazing women embracing their sexuality powerfully and positively with passion.

Contents

Editor's Note

As Jenna said in her great autobiography, *How to Make Love Like a Porn Star: A Cautionary Tale,* "Great sex begins in the mind." Then it travels.

Really sexy stories get inside your mind, get you off, make you laugh, and, hopefully, sometimes give you new ideas. These erotic stories were chosen not because of a common theme but because each is uncommon, each unique, each original. Just like we are as women.

As editor, I focused on choosing smart, funny, creative stories. Stories that might make you laugh out loud, or wish you could have thirty uninterrupted minutes, or make you have to call your best friend to share, or give you an idea of something you'd like to try.

It was also my goal to find stories with powerful sexy women in control, even when submissive. Women doing what they want to do, with *whom* they want to do it. It just seemed right for a collection of stories with Jenna Jameson as the inspiration.

Enjoy the stories, let them get your mind off—off your shopping lists, off your crappy day, off your bills to be paid, just off!

Knowing some of you (all of you) will try at least one thing from the book, whether it's a position, a place, a costume, or a role, JennaTips—Sex Tips for the Woman on Top—have been included. Notes and comments on the tales have also been included to let you know why a particular story was chosen, what set it apart.

You've no doubt whispered fantasies to your lovers—talked dirty, telling them all the little things you'd like to do with them. You've likely read them stories before. Read these to someone or download audio erotica at www.jennatales.com. Fantasy in bed (or the shower, or the backseat, or up against a wall . . .) is real and right. Fantasy takes good sex and makes it totally awesome.

Wishing you lots of great sex and love in your life.

—M. Catherine OliverSmith

Something Blue

If you feel like a sports widow, then find ways to make the game fun. Wear your team colors, cheer loud and long, and celebrate victories with wild, crazy sex. And if you lose, commiserate with wild, crazy sex!

Pass Interference

It was going to be a party! Or that's what my boyfriend, Brian, told me. We rarely entertained because the place was not that big. I was totally excited by the prospect. That is to say, I was right up until Brian started talking about how much beer to buy and I noticed that there was a lot of beer and not a lot of anything else. Some chips, cheese dip, peanuts, and more beer. Then I noticed that Brian kept talking to his best friend Jax about the "Big Game" and I finally figured out there wasn't going to be a party. It was going to be an entire afternoon of Brian and Jax sitting on the couch and me making small talk with some random new girlfriend of Jax's about her split ends and my new shoes until our brains shut down, and we just sat in silence waiting to be reanimated by the guys when the game ended.

The day arrived. *Whoopee.* I was chilling down the beer when Brian answered the knock at the door. I heard palms slap and some laughing. I pushed my hair behind my ears and went out to meet our guests.

Jax and Brian have been best friends forever and are like two peas in a pod personality-wise, which surprises lots of people since they appear to be polar opposites. Brian is pale white with a flattop, blond hair, and icy blue eyes. Built like a football player, he's all thick muscles and broad chest. Jax has caramel-brown skin and hazel eyes, sports braids down to his shoulders. Where Brian's broad, Jax is lithe, lean, and wiry like a marathoner or triathlete.

I'd met Jax many times and knew him pretty well as Brian's best friend, but I was meeting this girlfriend for the first time, as she was a fairly new addition. Introduced as Jess, she didn't look like Jax's type, based on past women I'd met. He seemed to go for women with some meat, with extra bits here and there. But Jess was almost as tall and slender as he was. Her skin was pale and eyes green—a contrast to her dark brown hair. I almost swallowed my tongue, she was so stunning. I finally managed to say hello like a normal person.

She had incredibly long legs and her skinny jeans just emphasized that they led to an incredibly slender waist and flat tummy. I'd say I was jealous, but while I might never be on a runway, I'm definitely a dangerous-curves-ahead kind of woman.

"Want to help make sandwiches?" I asked Jess with a smile. Her face wrinkled up as she looked at me with one eye closed.

"Um, sure. I guess," she wavered.

I led Jess into the kitchen as the guys set themselves up in front of the television. We chatted, light talk, while I used a sharp knife to cut the edges off a stack of sliced bread.

"You're cutting the crusts off for them?" Jess was amazed. "How ridiculous is that?"

I beamed. "Brian calls me his 'perfect little girlfriend.'"

"And you're proud of that?" Jess stuck a finger in her throat and pretended to heave.

"I've been called worse. I don't mind." Brian worked hard at a good job. He paid most of the bills. He didn't cheat and he rarely raised his voice. If he wanted me to cut the crusts off his sandwiches, I had no problem with it. He went out in the middle of the night to buy me ice cream when I had a craving without complaint, and rubbed my feet anytime I asked, so I thought of it as give-and-take.

I grabbed cold cuts and slices of cheese from the fridge and started combining them with the bread.

"Ooh, can I help?" Jess seemed suddenly eager.

I nodded and she leapt to the task. First, she gathered up all the crusts that I'd cut off. Then, she stuffed them between the cheeses and cold cuts.

"With enough mustard and mayo," she explained. "They'll never notice."

My eyebrows rose as I watched her sabotage my sandwiches. But I couldn't control my laughter. Jess was a serious pain in the ass. And I liked it.

I used a butter knife to splash mayo and mustard in the sandwiches. Put them all on a tray and walked toward the guys. In the living room, they'd moved the couch to within a couple inches of the television and were already hypnotized by pregame chatter. Brian didn't even bother to thank me when I set the sandwich tray on his lap. Maybe Jess was right. Maybe he was starting to take me for granted.

While Brian and Jax were captivated by the screen, Jess and I chatted at the kitchen table. Before long, we knew each other's astrological signs, favorite colors, musical preferences, and even how many pets we'd ever owned. And we played that game— you know, pet name plus street name is your porn name. Her porn name was Zsa Zsa Main and mine, I know you won't believe it, was Fat Bonnie Fair Way.

It was obvious that we were both getting very bored.

"How long does a game last?" Jess began to pick at her fingernails.

I shrugged my shoulders. I had no idea. I normally didn't stick around for game day and Brian rarely planned them at our place but would go out to a sports bar and be gone all day and lots of times most of the night. I didn't mind. I'd have a girls' night out, see a movie, sit on the couch like a blob and veg, whatever.

The place isn't really big and we could hear the game from where we sat. Finally I suggested we just go ahead and join the guys.

"Want to try watching the game? It wouldn't hurt to learn a bit about it. Maybe it'll be interesting."

There was a short pause before we both broke into hysterical laughter. Then, suddenly, Jess's lips twisted up at the corner and I swear I saw the gears turning behind her eyes as she planned something. Didn't take long for me to find out what.

"Watch this," she whispered as she reached under her shirt and writhed around while taking off her bra. Then she moved to the living room's entrance and tossed the garment on the floor in front of the television.

The guys didn't say a word. I don't think they noticed it at all. Jess wasn't upset. Instead, she seemed to take it as a challenge.

While I watched from the entry, she sauntered into the living room. The guys were hunched forward like desert vultures. Jess stepped directly between them and the television. She shook her ass directly in Jax's face as she pretended to pick her bra up off the ground.

The guys did an amazing job of ignoring her, which pissed her off a little. So my new friend suddenly whipped her shirt over her head, and thrust her chest out. Wagging her pert breasts and cocoa-colored nipples, she stretched her arms out to the sides— as though waiting for applause.

All Brian and Jax did was crane their necks to the sides so they could see around her.

Jess stomped away, and we met back in the kitchen.

"Nice try." I was impressed with her bravery. And not at all jealous since neither guy appeared to have noticed her in the least.

"Your turn." She was serious.

"What? Take my shirt off?" I wasn't so certain it was a good idea to show Jax my body. Brian and I might never see Jess again, since Jax's friends weren't generally long term, but I knew I'd see Jax again and again, and I didn't know if I could show him my boobs and not feel weird or create a problem with Brian.

"Come on. You have bigger tits. It might work," she insisted.

"I can't."

"You chicken?" She clucked while sticking her elbows out at her side like bony wings and dancing around the kitchen.

I was. But I wouldn't admit it. So I strode back into the living and faced the guys while I quickly pulled my T-shirt off, exposing my lacy push-up bra. You'd think that I wouldn't need a push-up, but my girls liked the extra support. It felt good to free myself from the uncomfortable underwire. Closing my eyes, I shook off the straps and threw it on the couch between them.

They looked as though they could see right through me. Silently, Brian waved a hand sideways to usher me out of his way.

"Forget it." I turned and almost knocked Jess over when I stormed back into the kitchen. My face collided with her chest, and one of my boobs hit her arm.

"Sorry," we both said at the same time. We exchanged grins as we left the guys to their stupid game.

Back in the kitchen, bras forgotten, we conspired on our next move when Brian called for more beers. I grabbed a couple of cans and stepped into the living room. Just far enough so I could toss them the brews. When I turned around, Jess's nose was touching mine.

"This'll get them," she whispered as she unsnapped her jeans and let them drop. With one foot, she kicked the pants back into the kitchen. Then she started working on my belt.

"Whoa." I backed away, but she tugged on the belt until I was back in her face. I was about to protest when my words, and my lips, were smothered by her kiss. I pulled back in surprise, and Jess grabbed my face with both hands. Closing my eyes, I enjoyed the soft feel of her mouth, the way she tasted like strawberry lipgloss and mint. When I parted my lips, her warm tongue filled my mouth, teasing me. When she moved her mouth to my neck, we were both breathing hard.

"Think that got their attention?" Jess licked my earlobe.

"Who cares?" I said, pushing her backward into the kitchen. I caught her when she stumbled, then pressed her ass against the kitchen table as we kissed again.

As I tasted her lovely mouth, I felt her hand between my legs, prying my thighs apart. She touched me with slick fingers until I was moaning. I pressed her onto the table until she was lying down with her legs bent and knees in the air. It was my first time with a woman since I was a LUG—Lesbian Until Graduation. But it was just like riding a bicycle. I didn't forget how. My tongue wandered from her navel to her lovely, plump lips, and finally to her delicious center. Jess gripped my head with her long thighs as I licked her, teasing her clit with slow movements.

I didn't even notice that the guys had finally joined us until I felt Brian behind me. He reached around to cup my breasts and pinch my nipples. Jax grinned at me before giving Jess a passionate kiss. Then he scooped her up and lay her down on the floor. I soon joined her as Brian positioned himself on top of me.

Finally. We'd stolen the guys' attention away from that damn game.

I looked over to see Jax slide on top of Jess, covering her torso with his lean body. She bit her lip as he entered her. At nearly the same time, Brian entered me. I was already wet from playing with Jess and his cock easily slipped in.

I stared at the ceiling, grunting with each hard stroke, until I felt fingertips brushing my hand. It was Jess, reaching out for me. I clasped onto her hand as a smile lit her face. Our eyes locked onto each other as Brian and Jax fucked us deep. Her grip tightened, her eyes fixed onto mine, she began to moan softly. And that set me off. Brian, sensing I was close, thrust harder.

I think I came first. Loud and long as Jess's fingers intertwined with mine. Soon after, I heard her moans stretching out soft and sweet. My thighs were sticky with sweat and come as I tried to catch my breath. I met Jess's glance and saw the same just-fucked grin on her face. I returned her wink and giggle. We were proud. We'd done the impossible. We'd gotten our men away from football.

Before my breath had a chance to calm, the guys were moving. Jax hopped over to the fridge as he wiggled back into his pants. He nabbed a jar of cheese dip. Brian, twisting his shirt across his wide shoulders and chest, found chips in the cupboard. Then, in single file, they began marching back toward the living room.

"Where you going?" I called after them.

Brian turned back to explain. "Half-time's over! The game's starting up again!"

Ellen Doyle

JennaTip #1: Getting Your Game On

Game Day! Or game season! Or for some of you—all damn year long! Don't get pissy and mad if he likes watching the game or games. Talk about it and set some reasonable limits, but understand this may be the one way he really relaxes (other than sex). It's also a way for him to bond with other guys. Let's face it, guys can really suck at friendship, because they just don't know how to talk. So give him his sports, but get something for you, too.

One way to deal with the whole sports fascination is to get into the sport, too. It'll be much better if you can watch and cheer along with him. Throughout the game, plan on having great celebration sex or great consolation sex once it's over. This way you can look at the game as foreplay. Bet on the score with the prize being something you want. You know, a kiss here or a kiss there, maybe some deep kisses everywhere! Make watching the game fun for both of you.

Another idea is that if there is a fumble by his team, then he does something for you—a neck massage, a deep kiss, some nice tongue action the next commercial time-out—and if his team intercepts a pass, then he gets a treat of his choice. Things like this can make the game more fun, and you might actually get his attention away from the game altogether.

You can also get into the whole game day by picking out some sexy underwear or painting your body in the team colors. You could try dressing up as a cheerleader (or a player). Your guy is likely to find it seriously hot to see his woman in a team jersey and not much else. Smudge under your eyes and go get the ball(s)!

A good hard fuck against the public bathroom stall is a great way to relieve tension. It's also a good icebreaker with a new friend.

The Viper's Loving Embrace

She floated into the bar like there were wheels under her feet. Off-blond hair, not too tall. Mysterious dark eyes. She wore a blue tank and tight, matching soccer shorts. She was made of muscle and sinew. Like she spent her lifetime at the gym. Broad shoulders and thick arms, she could have looked manly, but she had curves in all the right places. Lean and muscular, but still feminine.

I doubted that I was the only guy incapable of taking his eyes away from her. She sat a few bar stools away from me. Near enough that I could get a nice view. But far enough away that approaching her would be uncomfortable—especially when she turned her well-defined back toward me.

She ordered tonic water from the bartender and sipped it through a red straw. I'd never once been close to a woman, intimately close, who was in such amazing shape. She was stunning. Like punch-to-the-head stunning. I could barely focus, at least on anything else. I couldn't help but imagine how her shoulders and thighs would feel to my touch. How hard her body would be and, in contrast, how soft her skin. Of course I knew it was just a daydream.

I was jealous, almost, when another guy approached her. He must have weighed twice as much as her and was nearly twice as old. In shape—not. He sported a rolling belly and extra chin.

9

"I know you!" He pointed at her.

"You do?" Her voice matched his tone and pitch.

"From the TV," he belched into his fist. "You wrestle."

She didn't answer. She didn't have to. But I had an *A-ha*! moment myself as I finally recognized her. She was a new challenger, up and coming, described as very focused. And cold, stone cold.

Her silence didn't stop him. "You are one sexy lady. Want to join my friends and me?" His head cocked back to a table where his two sneering, idiot buddies were sitting.

"No," was all she said. One word that meant a lot.

I was relieved. I wasn't done daydreaming about her yet. Then again, if I got enough balls up to approach her, would I get the same chilly, one-word reply?

"What? You too good for me?" The guy didn't understand what "no" meant. "Stuck-up bitch."

I thought of jumping to her defense. But that went against my golden rule: don't intervene. It's not my job to put myself in the middle. I play it straight. I play it safe. I play it simple. And I mind my business and let others take care of their own.

She didn't say another word. But the guy wouldn't let it go. "You're fake. Wrestling is fake, and so are you." Then he pushed too far when his pointed finger jabbed her in the arm.

She reacted immediately. Her hand lashed out, grabbed his wrist, and twisted it back while one of her feet jabbed at the hollow of his knee. The guy screamed as he fell, back-first, to the floor. A moment later she had a knee on his chest and a foot on his free arm.

She still didn't say a word.

His buddies kicked out of their chairs and moved fast toward her. I guess that even golden rules are meant to be broken. All she'd done was walk into a bar. She wasn't looking for any problems. She was just looking for a drink. I sure as shit wasn't going to sit and watch while three goons jumped her.

The guy's buddies stopped when I hopped in front of them. Now, I'm no tough guy. I'm more of a spectator than a participant, a watcher, not a fighter. They looked me over and spit air through their noses, knowing that I couldn't stop them alone. There were at least a dozen other guys in that place and not one of them dared or cared enough to offer any help.

"Okay! Okay," I heard the guy on the floor. His voice was different than before. Higher pitched, more apologetic. He knew she'd beaten him but good. She let him up and he waved for his partners to follow him out of that place. I hoped no one noticed how much I was shaking.

She was sitting on her chair and sipping through her red straw again even before I'd caught my breath. I stuffed my hand in a pocket, crossed my fingers, and moved up to her.

"That was a sweet move," I complimented.

"Thanks. First thing they taught us in wrestling college." She winked and I laughed.

"C-can I," I stuttered. ". . . buy you a drink?"

"No alcohol tonight. I have a big match tomorrow. Biggest of my career so far. I need to be clear and complete."

Well, at least I got better than the one word "no" that the other guy got. I started moving back to my seat.

"But you can sit with me for a while, if you want," she invited.

I sat and offered her my hand. "I'm Bob."

She took my hand gently and wiggled it a little.

"Your name?" I asked.

"Stage or real?"

"Your real name."

"Eve," she answered with a smile. But suddenly she seemed distracted.

"Something wrong?" I was breaking my golden rule again. But she was worth it.

"Nothing, really." She was a bad liar. "Okay, it's the match tomorrow. Big break for me. But I'm up against a real bitch. Highly ranked. And she's known to cheat a lot."

"Cheat? How can she do that?"

"Lots of practice. She hides coin rolls in her waistband and uses them when she punches. And I hear she even has a pair of steel-toed sneakers. I swear, the refs are blind, deaf, and dumb some days."

"Handle her like you did that guy a few minutes ago. You'll do fine." I tried to comfort her.

"Thanks." She laughed again. "I just hope tomorrow's ref pays attention. It's all up to him. If he keeps it a fair match until I can spring my signature move on her, I'll kick her ass."

"Signature move?" I was curious.

"Well, it will be my signature move. If it works. I call it the Viper's Loving Embrace." She grabbed a napkin and the bartender's pencil and sketched the scene for me with stick figures.

"Check it out," she explained. "Off the top rope, I do a semi-flip and wrap my legs around her neck. My crotch is against her face, and my face is in her lap. You know, like she's giving me a piledriver. My hands grip her thighs, and the momentum pulls her down to her knees. A twist one way, then the other. A tug and a pull later her shoulders are on the mat and the ref is slapping his palm red." She dropped the pencil onto the bar and awaited my reaction.

She was an impressive woman. Strong, smart, and sexy. I looked at the stick figures on the napkin.

"It seems oddly erotic," I said. She laughed at my discomfort.

"I've heard it said that wrestling is a lot like fucking, except with a big audience and small clothes," Eve smiled. Then she used the red straw to suck at the bottom of her glass. "Mmm. I could use a couple of real drinks. Just to relax some."

"I won't tell anyone if you do."

She shook her head. "Nah. I have to be on top for tomorrow. Too bad I broke up with my boyfriend last month. Sex is an even better stress-reliever than booze."

We sat quietly for a while. She spent the time rolling what was left of the ice around the bottom of her glass as I tapped my fingers on the bar.

"How about if—" I started, then stopped. Her eyes narrowed and her thin brows rose as she watched my mouth.

"Could I . . . I mean . . . maybe we . . ." I tried again and again, with each attempt making me more nervous and embarrassed. Eve giggled against her index finger as her lips puckered. She was making me work for this. I inhaled deep.

"I could help?" Damn. It came out as a question instead of a statement. "Volunteer. Stress relief, you know? Me . . . With you, like—" I don't know how it happened without me noticing, but someone had obviously nailed my tongue to the top of my mouth.

"I never thought you'd offer." She placed a palm on my thigh. "Where do we go? I share my hotel room with another gal."

"I have a roommate," I confessed. "His girlfriend is over for the night. That's why I'm here."

Eve flicked her straw with a finger and carefully scanned the bar. The bartender had stepped into the back room and the all-male crowd was engaged with chatter and drinks.

"Follow me." She stood and motioned to the back wall. I obeyed, marveling at my good luck. When she reached the door to the women's restroom, she glanced back at the bar. Seeing that no one was watching, she grabbed my arm and yanked me inside with her.

I'd never really seen the inside of a women's room before, at least not after I was six or seven and absolutely refused to go with my mother any longer. It was a damn sight cleaner than the guys'. No toilet paper on the floor or graffiti on the walls. Of course, no urinals either. And I swear that the air smelled like lavender.

Eve rested her butt against the sink and crossed her arms. "I'm the only woman in the bar. We should be okay in here. For a few minutes at least."

I froze. I just stood there. I couldn't get my legs to budge.

Eve looked at me impatiently. "I said a few minutes, Bob. Not a few hours."

Two steps later and she bruised my lips with hers. Her palms on my shoulders, she pushed up until her ass was on top of the sink. As we kissed, she trapped me when her legs wrapped around my waist. My fingers stroked her tight thighs, as smooth as they were buff. She grabbed my hand and swiftly slipped it into her shorts. She was wet, and it was easy for one of my fingers to enter. Sighing, she reached down and grabbed my hard-on. She squeezed, just tight enough for my cock to grow and fill her palm.

Our tongues tangled as she backed me into one of the stalls, forcing me to sit. Straddling me, she ground herself onto my lap. I moved my hands up her shirt, feeling the firm muscles in her stomach and chest. Her breasts—not too big, not tiny— were natural and tender. When she tore her top off, she pushed a nipple into my mouth and clasped my ears.

I ran my hands all over her hard body, enjoying her firm, tight flesh. I thought it would be weird being with such a well-defined woman. She had a better body than I did. Much more definition. Yet she was the perfect combination of hard edge and soft femininity.

She stood and pushed down her pants, then her thong. Pointing at my front, she said, "Pants off. Now."

It didn't take me long to obey. I returned to my seat as she settled on top of me. She was so wet that I slid into her in one smooth motion. I massaged her thighs and tight ass as she slowly rocked against me.

The slow motion became faster until she was bucking wildly, her breasts bouncing in front of my face. Once in a while, I'd reach out with my tongue, flicking a nipple and tasting her soft skin.

Emboldened by the action and my inflated cock, I grabbed her by the ass and managed to stand. Pressing her back against the stall door, I fucked her standing up, driving into her with hard thrusts. My knees burned and my legs trembled. But I fucked her until she was screaming my name over and over. I came right after she did. Both of our voices were hoarse from all the grunting and moaning.

I felt a lot more relaxed walking out of that restroom than I had walking in. Eve's smile showed that she felt the same. At the bar, we talked for a few more minutes. Then, suddenly, she shook my hand, planted a small kiss on my cheek, and left.

I was sad to see her go.

But I knew I'd see her again.

The next evening the crowd was in a roaring mood. They hooted, booed, and clapped for no reason at all. Eve looked stunning as she passed from the halls and into the spotlights. Unlike some of the other wrestlers, she didn't wear an elaborate costume. No mask, no sequins. Nothing that would distract attention from her defined muscles. Her black leotard showed off her firm biceps and legs. The V-neck of her tight top exposed her cleavage.

With her eyes glued on her opponent, Eve paced slowly around the ring, like a predator stalking her prey. Then she leapt toward the corner and got on the second rope. She raised her head, her fist slowly rising in the air. Turning to her opponent, she slid her thumb across her throat. Venom dripped from her eyes.

The crowd went crazy.

When she returned to the center of the ring, she noticed me for the first time. I was the guy in black and white, standing in the center. That's right. I reffed her match.

I was tempted to call it all her way. But that was against my occasionally broken but never forgotten golden rule.

Oh, and Eve's signature move, The Viper's Loving Embrace?

It worked even better in the ring than it did on a napkin.

Bev Ichan

Put a leash on it and you have yourself your very own Pet Cock.

She Might as Well Name It

My Gloria loves my cock. I don't just mean she's hot to fuck it and suck it and take it up her ass. She's into all that, but she's crazy for my cock just to look at and pet. Best of all, she likes to watch me come. I think that to her I'm just the guy my cock is attached to. She even met my cock before she met me. It was like this . . .

You know what it's like straphanging in a commuter train in rush hour? You get squished in on all sides by all those bodies. Sometimes you get some chick in front of you with her ass pushed back against you and what with the pushing and shoving and the train rocking, it gets embarrassing. Your hard-on is rubbing against her even though you pull back and hold still, but there's nothing you can do about it. You get scared she's gonna think you're doing it deliberately and will get pissed and call a transit cop. At the same time, you're half getting off on it.

I was on the way home when I got jammed up tight behind Gloria but I didn't know her, not then. The carriage was packed. She had on this, like, real thin dress so my woody could feel the heat of her ass through it and my jeans. Every time the train swayed it was like I was fucking between her cheeks. Someone behind me moved, so I was able to back off about three inches. She stayed with me and pressed against me even harder. I didn't believe it at first. She gave a bit of a wriggle back at me. Then I believed it. I tried a bit of a hump at her, testing. She humped her answer. I thought, *Oh fuck, I got lucky!*

The next thing was unbelievable! Gloria reached back behind her and started fumbling with my zipper. In about five seconds flat she had my fly open and her hot little hand groping inside. I felt her fingers stroke up and down my shaft, checking it out. She must have liked what she felt 'cause she made a fist around me and started slow-pumping. I want her to keep on doing what she's doing, but what about when I came? I'd have me jeans full of come. I leaned down—she's short, my Gloria—and I whispered into her ear, "My stop is next."

She goes, "It's my stop, too. When we get off, I'll get you off." She gave me a squeeze, let me go, and left me to pull my own zipper up.

I got out close behind her to hide my bulge. She walked ahead, fast, so I had to hurry to keep up. "You need to make a phone call," she called over her shoulder.

There was a pay phone with a cubicle that's got a door but it only came down to about the middle of my thighs. She bundled me in. "Make like you're calling someone," she said.

I picked up the phone and pretended to dial. She was tight in next to me, facing out, mostly hiding me from all the commuters rushing by outside. One hand comes round in front of me, yanks my zipper down again, pulls my cock out, and starts jerking it again. I said, "We could get caught!"

She said, "Yeah!" and worked me faster.

"When I come—what'll we do with my jism?"

"Don't worry about it." Her fist went faster.

I gasped, "I'm gonna . . ."

She twisted round, got her other hand in front of me, and took my hot load right into her cupped palm. I was groaning, weak at the knees, when she put her hand up to her mouth and sucked all the jism off it.

"Lovely," she said, licking white blobs off her lips.

"I know you!" I said.

"Yeah—our folks' yards back onto each other. Handy, right?"

And that's how we started going together. It was like that from then on. Gloria couldn't keep her hands off my cock, and she liked to do it in public. That scared me some but I was getting my load drained all the time, so I didn't complain none.

The first time we went and parked up at the Point and got into the back of my old Buick, I found she'd brought a flashlight. That's what she used to check me out. I must have sat there with my cock out and her looking at it and fondling it for about an hour before she started stroking me off again. I said, "I'm gonna come, Gloria! Go down on me, babe."

"Next time, I promise. This time I want to watch." She caught my load in a tissue that she put in her purse. "For under my pillow, so I can smell you. Now let's see how fast you can come again." She timed me with her watch. First she just toyed with my limp cock, flopping it from side to side and running her thumb up the underside, then she got serious, licking its head like it was ice cream, finally working on it as she sucked and took my load right in her mouth.

"Eleven minutes," she said, looking at her watch. "I guess the next one will take longer."

She got me off six times in an hour and fifty-four minutes, by her timing. By then all I could manage was a trickle of clear fluid. She'd, like, totally drained my fucking balls!

I slept real well that night but about three in the A.M., I was woken by someone tapping at my window. My folks' place is a ranch-style so my bedroom is at ground level. I went over and

looked out. It was her, standing on the ground outside. I pushed
the window up and leaned out. "What is it?" I asked.

"Shh! Put your cock out and then pull the window back
down."

So I did. It felt strange, me inside and my cock poking outside. My knob felt cold but not for long. Warm lips closed over
it. Her tongue got to work on my knob. Gloria started into
sucking and bobbing her head. My balls must have recovered by
then 'cause in about five minutes I came again. I pulled up the
window to thank her but she was already gone.

We used to do it in the woods near where we lived. We'd lay
in the grass and make out for a while but it always ended with
her checking my cock out with her eyes, hands, and mouth.
Once in a while we'd fuck, but when we did she always wanted
me to pull out so she could watch me come. Sometimes she'd
make daisy chains and wrap them around my shaft. Other times
she stroked it with blades of grass, asking me, "Can you feel it
when I do this? How about this?" One time she worked a blade
into the eye of my cock and tried to twirl it around but it just
broke off. I was worried about getting the end out but Gloria
managed to suck it out.

Once we went up to where the highway crosses Ridge River.
With four lanes of traffic whizzing by, she had me lean on the
rail, looking down at the brown swirling water, while she reached
through and slow-jerked me till I shot a supersize order of cream
down onto the water. She said as how it looked so cute, my
frothy come floating away on the waves.

We double-dated some with Jan and Ed. Jan's folks are pretty
nice. The four of us went to "watch TV" in their rec room, in
the basement. It was fine by them if we made out, though Jan's
mom kept checking on us, bringing pop and so on, just to see
we kept to suck-tonguing and groping the girls' tits through

their sweaters. She was okay with the girls sitting on our laps as long as we had our hands up where she could see 'em.

I was getting pretty horny, what with Gloria wriggling on my hard-on. After a while, Gloria got up, pulled her full-circle skirt out from between us, and sat down on me again. With that skirt flared out I was covered by it from my waist to my knees. I figured she had something in mind. She did. Her hand worked between us and got my cock out.

I said, "Jan's mom might come in."

"She won't see nothing. I got a treat for you."

I didn't have to wonder what my treat would be for long. Gloria wormed around on me, sliding my cock against the smooth cheeks of her ass till she got it in the crack. That's when I realized she had no panties on. "You know what I was thinking about that day we met on the train?" she asked me.

"I dunno."

"This," she said, and lifted up a bit.

My cock's head was right in the crack of her ass. She lowered herself. It felt like my cock came to a dead end but she slowly humped and twisted and pushed down. I popped right in, right into her ass! At first it was just the head, then slowly she moved about and I slid on in. It was my first time. My cock wanted me to shove and shove but how the fuck could I? My cock was buried in that tight, hot passage and I didn't dare move.

Jan's mom came in with milk and cookies. When she offered them to Gloria, my girl leaned forward to take them. My cock don't bend easy when it's hard, but it did then. I was pretty much in shock. There I was, sitting on the couch, my cock up Gloria's tight little ass, and Gloria was chatting away to Jan's mom like nothing was going on.

Jan's mom left. Gloria said, "Jan, there's nothing on TV. Why don't you put something on the CD and we can listen to music?"

Jan did. Something with a solid beat came on, which was all the excuse Gloria needed. Sitting on my cock, she started rocking to the music, slowly at first, then after a bit she started really bouncing up and down, swinging her hips. I came in about no time. Good job Gloria was twisted round and sucking on my tongue or I'd have made some sort of noise. When she felt my cock fill her ass with my jism, calm as anything, Gloria reached for her bag, got a tissue, lifted off me and stuffed the Kleenex up her ass. She zipped me up and in and said, "'Excuse me. I gotta go to the john."

So no one, not even Ed or Jan, sussed what we'd been doing, even though we'd done it right in front of them.

Gloria bought me a pair of jeans for my birthday. I thought the factory had made a mistake but when I told her, she said as how it was her what'd cut the pocket out. That way she could sneak a hand in and cop a feel whenever she felt like it.

"Whenever she felt like it" is all the fucking time. When we hang out at Burger King she gets extra napkins to stuff through my missing pocket so she can jerk me off with one hand while she eats fries with the other. When we go for a drive, she makes me drive with my cock out, just so she can look at it.

My cock gets spoiled. Gloria keeps skin lotion for it and carries talc in her purse in the summer to make sure it keeps cool and fresh. She buys it treats—chocolate sauce and the like. When we're alone, we don't neck so much no more. It's, "Get it out for me," then she's down there, talking to it, petting it, kissing it.

I guess I'm a lucky guy, right? Still, it ain't a perfect relationship. I mean, I'm a person, aren't I? There's more to me than my cock. My Gloria's wonderful, but sometimes I figure she might as well name it, put a leash on it, and take it for a walk.

Teri Canfield

JennaTip #2: Getting Behind Sex (pun intended)

Anal sex can be pretty awesome when done correctly. Make sure your partner starts off by loosening you up with fingers or tongue or mini-dildo or anal plug or whatever is hygienic first. This will make it easier and it should also be a ton of fun. The anus is a really tight area and for this to be good for you both, it must be lubed and it must be relaxed. If you are scared or stressed, then you'll clench and it won't go well.

Be sure to clean the area first, even the inside a bit. You may want to use an enema. After you are totally primed and ready, even begging, be sure he's rock hard. If you are using a strap-on or dildo, pick one that's a good size for you, maybe starting with something smaller and working your way up. Have your partner slowly insert the tip. Once the head is fully in, wait. Take a breath and relax. Enjoy that feeling before trying to slide all of it in. If too much pressure is used at the start and he slides home, you're going to be on the ceiling!

Once he's all the way in, again you will want to wait. Just enjoy the fullness of it all before you start with the whole moving in-and-out part. Rub your clit as it really enhances the whole experience and keeps you wet and lubed. Now is the time to start slowly with the in-and-out. Don't tense up! Use your nails to let him know when he's in too deep. Once you get comfortable . . . get it on! When done correctly, anal can be awesome.

If you are confused about how you use your nails, anal doesn't have to be doggy style. Lift your legs well up so your ass is high. Try putting your ankles on his shoulders, for example, or bring your knees up into your chest.

Scones and Moans

Emily had only been working with me for two weeks, and she was already getting on my last nerve. She was ambitious, but way too energetic. She wanted to do everything immediately, before she really understood what needed to be done. My biggest hurdle was that she just didn't appreciate things like recipes and measuring cups. Her lack of focus drove me crazy.

But she worked hard. More important, she was trustworthy. There were plenty of bakers in town who would pay hard cash for a glimpse at my secret recipes. I couldn't hire just anyone.

"I didn't think we'd be this busy," Emily explained why we were short of butter.

I rubbed my temples, but that didn't help at all. I couldn't yell at her because I didn't expect us to be this busy either. Ever since we were featured in the local newspaper's food section, we'd been swamped with new customers. Before the article, business had been going strong. All our goods were baked early in the morning and ready, fresh and warm, for the commuters and midmorning coffee break crowd.

My little shop used to be popular with just the locals, but now we were moving up. This wasn't just a coffee-and-treats joint anymore. Everyone, it seemed, wanted to try my scones.

I'm not trying to brag, but I do make a world-class scone. Part cookie and part biscuit, my scone doesn't require any cutesy additives. No chocolate, no raspberries, no preservatives, nothing artificial. Just a buttery scone that isn't too dry and isn't too chewy.

24

And, of course, the mojo: my own special batch of spices that is my secret. The one that gives my scones their special flavor.

I vigorously wiped down the counter with a damp cloth. I was a nut when it came to a clean kitchen, and some days I spent more time wiping, sweeping, and scrubbing than I did actually baking. My rag suddenly came across a small bag that a friend from college had dropped off a few days before. She was wild back then and hadn't tamed much in the years since.

She'd told me the bag contained a powerful aphrodisiac. She wanted me to mix up a special batch of chocolate cupcakes with it for an exclusive adult party she was planning. She invited me to attend, but it wasn't really my bag. I'd make the treats, however.

I'd put the bag on the top shelf and almost forgotten about it in the mad rush since our favorable review. I wasn't sure how it had found its way down to the counter, but I was too busy to worry about that. I just hid it back where it belonged and then went to the cash register in front.

It was busy for a Tuesday morning. With Gail out sick with the flu, I had to be both baker and cashier. Usually I didn't mind. I liked getting to know my customers.

Except one. Cathy was a blond attorney who worked in the adjacent building. Every day she came in for one scone and a black coffee. Strong and bitter, just like her. Every day it was the same order and the same bad attitude.

Today she decided that the coffee wasn't hot enough. I offered her a new cup, but she wanted hers freshly brewed.

I sighed and said, "You'll have to wait five minutes."

"Fine," she sneered, then sat at a small table near the window.

Some guy I hadn't seen before was next. He looked like a delivery guy who'd been up all night—more tired than sloppy. He ordered two almond bear claws, a scone, and a hot chocolate.

Then he moved over to the window and sat near the blond attorney. Like Felix and Oscar from *The Odd Couple*, I thought it
was interesting that two people so obviously from different
worlds could sit next to one another in my little shop.

After that was the young cop, Officer Beal. Tall, good-looking
in a bland, preppy sort of way. Short brown hair and brown eyes.
He couldn't have been more than twenty-one. Another regular.
He always had two scones. Ate one here and took one to go. He
smiled when I handed him his change. If only he were a bit
older . . . I won't go there.

Emily left a tray of fresh scones for the two couples waiting at
the corner table. They were chatting together in Vietnamese or
something. Their backpacks and laptops told me they were
probably students at the local college. The girls could have been
twins except one had way more curves than the other. From the
way the couples held hands and giggled, I guessed they hadn't
been dating long.

"Emily, I think you'll need to start another batch." I had the
feeling that lunchtime would be hectic as well.

Emily scooted past the register and toward the back. "The
scones taste different today. But good."

I knew it. I never should have let her mix the morning batch
by herself. "Follow the recipe," I demanded.

"I did this time! I swear." She winked at me before she dashed
back into the kitchen.

I was searching my purse for aspirin when I heard a strange
noise. I ignored it. But heard it again. Louder this time. It
sounded like a low moan.

This time I looked up. *What the hell?* The first thing I saw was
the back of Cathy's head, her blond hair flying as it bobbed up
and down on the delivery driver's lap. Had she lost her damn
mind?

The driver wrapped his fingers in her hair, pushed her head farther down. From the sounds of her gags, she was taking him deep. But she didn't seem to mind. If anything, his gestures excited her even more.

Officer Beal turned and walked toward the couple. I was so glad he was here to take care of this bizarre situation, but then he unzipped, reaching his hand into his fly. He took her pumping ass while keeping time with her head bobbing as an invitation. My jaw dropped the same time as his pants did. His thick cock pointed straight up and I could even see a drop of pre-come glistening on its tip.

"Stop that!" I finally found my voice. Officer Beal didn't listen. Instead he pushed Cathy's skirt up, exposing her lacy pink thong. I don't know what shocked me more: what was happening or the fact that she wore pink.

Outside, traffic was backing up from the red light at the corner, and some drivers turned away from their cell phones to spy inside the shop. I raced over and shut the window blinds halfway, and then the strings got tangled up. By the time I was able to drop the shades and turn around, the four students had their shirts off and were kissing. I was pretty sure they'd swapped partners.

"Cut it out!" I barked. But that only made them giggle. I thought of grabbing the fire extinguisher and cooling everyone off, but I saw the front door opening. Shit! The last thing I needed was another customer walking in.

I rushed to the door and pushed my shoulder against it as the mailman tried to deliver the day's bills.

"Hey!" he shouted.

"Sorry!" I slid the locks in place and flipped the Open sign to Closed. By the time I turned around, the party of three was lying on the floor. The blonde, in the middle of a stud sandwich, had lost her top and a high heel. Officer Beal spooned her, thrusting into her as she begged for more. The delivery guy didn't seem as tired anymore. His pants were off, shirt unbuttoned, and hands on Cathy's breasts as he slid his tongue all over her toned upper body.

The foursome was soon on the floor as well, their naked limbs tangled as they traded wet kisses. Girl on guy. Girl on girl. The curvy girl blew me a kiss as she got on all fours. Swiftly her current partner entered her from behind and her soft laughter turned into throaty moans.

Her original boyfriend took a position in front of her to fuck her mouth while the other girl played with her friend's bouncing breasts. Soon the women switched places like their movements had been rehearsed.

"Emily!" I screamed. I'd need her help to calm this place down. Help as in a broom and a bucket of ice water. When she didn't respond, I went back into the kitchen. I found her there, leaning over the sink. Her pants were down to her knees, panties pushed aside, and her skinny ass was trembling as she masturbated furiously.

Her, too? "Emily?"

"Oh, hi!" Her motions calmed a bit. "Can you give me a hand?"

Then I noticed the bag on the counter.

"What the hell is this doing out again?"

Emily, back to masturbating full speed, spoke between gasps, "That's for the scones, right? It's what I used."

That explained a lot. She'd been using the aphrodisiac in the scones that morning, rather than my spice mix.

Emily began moaning as her wild shaking calmed and became more deliberate. Suddenly she froze, allowing her orgasm to wash across her skin.

"How much did you use?" I asked.

"A cup, right?" she panted.

About ten times the required amount. "Get dressed," I snapped. "Drink coffee. Lots of it. Give away as much as you can to the customers." Then, as an afterthought I added, "And wash your hands!"

Since her paycheck seemed more important than carnal pleasures, Emily washed up, poured herself a coffee, and then brought the pot out to the front. I started brewing more. I didn't know if coffee would help. But what else could I do?

By the time another pot was ready, the shop had cooled down a lot. The sex scenes were over. The blond attorney had straightened up enough to smooth out her clothes and was now walking toward the door. It was the first time I'd seen a smile on her face. The delivery guy watched with an unlit cigarette sticking out of his mouth. Officer Beal was having a hard time buckling his belt, and I think he lost a flashlight.

The four college students were all properly dressed and sitting in front of their coffee cups. They were a lot more quiet now than when they'd first come in. But each one of them wore a wide grin. And now all four of them held hands in one long link.

The place was a mess. A pair of panties hung off the ceiling fan. Icing was smeared on the counters and tables and crumbs littered the floor. And Emily seemed to have poured as much coffee outside of the cups as she'd poured into them. I handed the fresh pot to Emily and told her to keep passing out the brew and then to clean the place up.

I went back into the kitchen to hide the secret ingredient when I heard a light tap against the rear door. Opening it an inch, I saw the local health inspector, an attractive guy with dark, brown hair and gleaming blue eyes. Sneak inspection. He'd probably been checking out the vents and Dumpster outside. And now he wanted a look inside.

Son of a bitch.

The kitchen was clean and up to code. But the front was still a mess and my horny customers were still calming down. It would be professional suicide if I let him see the place the way it was. But he had the authority. If I locked him out, he'd shut me down for sure. *Ouch.*

I invited him in and offered him a tray, taking one pastry for myself.

"Would you like a scone?" I asked with a wink and a smile.

Heather Willis

Go ahead and laugh your ass off! Sex is fun, creative, hot, and when it's all of that and more at the same time, it's AWESOME! Enjoy!

The Good Wife

It was my dream wedding. A short and sweet ceremony followed by a rocking reception. We only stayed for a couple of hours. After that, Nick and I, husband and wife, went straight to our room. A five-star honeymoon suite complete with a bottle of chilled champagne and so many fresh flowers that the place smelled like a spring garden.

"Now this is the life." Moving in view of the bathroom mirror, I pulled the pins from my hair and shook out my blond curls.

Nick stepped behind me and whispered against my neck. "Let me help you out of that gown." His nervous fingers began fumbling with the back zipper and a few moments later, he was pushing the lace gown over my shoulders. "You're so beautiful," he said on seeing my matching white bra and white lace thong.

I'm not usually a big fan of white lingerie, but it was my wedding night. I also figured it played into Nick's whole fantasy thing. It had been great fun for our courtship to hold off on the sex so we could have this amazing night of discovery, and I was dressed for the part. The only problem was my wet, aching pussy just wasn't willing to maintain the charade.

"You look amazing," he said when I turned to face him. Then he just stood there, like he wanted to study me all night.

"Why don't we check out the bedroom?" I really wasn't in that much of a hurry. Okay. I lie. I wanted to rip off his clothes right there. But I love Nick. If he wants a wedding night, then he's getting one.

Like a gentleman, he carried me to the bed and laid me on top of the plush covers. He kissed me gently. Softly. Like we were kissing for the first time. I grabbed his hand and put it on my breast. I can only put up with so much of this fantasy. Arching my back, I moaned when he caressed my nipple.

He kissed the side of my neck and returned to my lips. He was still hesitant. Well, I just wasn't having any of it. I pushed his shoulder until he got the hint. When he rolled onto his back, I straddled him.

"I want to be on top." I tossed my bra onto the floor.

"You do?" Nick play-acted surprise, but his hardening cock told me he liked the idea. Grinding my hips, I rubbed my body against him. Leaning back, I let him get a good view of all of me.

He touched my panties and smiled. "God, you're so wet."

"I am." I sighed, deeply. "And what are you doing about that?"

He slid the lace to the side and touched me. "Does that feel good?"

"Yes." I lifted my hips to give him better access.

"How does this feel?" He entered me with a finger. "That hurt?"

"Not at all, baby. That feels so good." My panties were already soaked, and I wanted him inside me. The slow tease was nice, but I wanted more. I stood on the mattress and slid my thong down my hips. Nice and slow so he could enjoy the show. Once I was completely nude, he scrambled out of his clothes and tossed them on the floor. When he was back down on his back, his thick cock was pointing at me.

"Are you sure you don't want me to be on top? I mean, maybe it . . ." The rest of his sentence became a long groan as I straddled him again, guiding his cock inside me. Then I leaned back and rested my hands on his legs and rode him like an expert. I fucked that new husband of mine until his eyes rolled back into his forehead.

It was fantastic. I am so glad that I hadn't given in and had sex with him. Not once. In two years.

By the time I was done with him, he was screaming my name. "Jessica . . . Jessica . . . Jessica. . . ." I collapsed, breathless, onto his chest, the wild beating of our hearts making our bodies tremble.

And then Nick, in all seriousness, said, "Wow. That was incredible. I can't believe you can fuck like that. Your first time and all."

I tilted my head and peeked into his eyes. "Can't we stop with the damn fantasy now?"

"Fantasy?" Nick looked confused.

"Yes. The damn I'm-a-saint-and-virgin fantasy," I moaned.

Nick just blinked several times, shaking his head as though he'd just been hit between the eyes with a ballpeen hammer.

"Nick. You know it's not my first time. We're married. I'm glad we didn't have sex with each other. I think that made the wedding night thing seem real and the sex, I have to say, is fabulous. But I am tired of pretending. I need to just be real from now on."

Nick's body stiffened as he slowly turned to me. "For the two years we dated, every time I asked if you'd slept with anyone before, you said no."

I slid off him as he sat up like a shot. "You are so silly. Of course I said I never slept with anyone before. It was part of your fantasy. Additionally, I have to say, it wasn't even a lie. No one ever had the time to sleep. And I don't count people passing out as sleep."

It was very quiet for almost a minute while Nick's mind processed this new information. Then he asked again. "You mean you aren't a virgin?" His voice sounded betrayed.

"Of course not," I answered.

Nick swung his feet off the bed, stood, found his slacks, and wiggled into them.

"Nick." I tried to get his attention.

"You should have told me the truth." He looked like a sad lost puppy.

"Maybe you should have asked the right question. I thought you knew all along." He wasn't going to blame all this on me.

Nick found his shirt and struggled to put it on. I noticed it was inside out and that he was mismatching the buttons.

"How many?" He was turning angry. "How many did you fuck?"

I was getting angry, too. "Probably no more than you," I spat.

"I've been with five women," he confessed.

"Wow." I was surprised. No, really. I was stunned. I thought for sure he had more experience than that.

"Now. How about you?"

I didn't have the exact number in my head, so I tried to quickly count names, but then remembered that I didn't know all their names.

"Well, let's just say more than you but fewer than you could fit on a bus." I didn't want to be caught in a lie, so I added, "You know, one of those double-decker buses, like in London?"

Nick turned red, so red that you could probably fry an egg on his face.

"Did I know any of them?" he demanded.

Oh. Now that was going to be a tough question to answer. But I figured it was best to be honest.

"Well, there was Tom."

"Tom? My best man Tom?"

"Yeah, him. That Tom."

"When did you sleep with that Tom?

"About a week ago."

"A week ago!" he practically screamed.

"You know, the night of your bachelor party."

"My bachelor party?"

"Yes, your bachelor party." I figured a little reminder might jog his memory. "The night you let that stripper give you a lap dance and then a blow job in front of all your friends."

That shut Nick up. He couldn't even look at me after that. So I kept on. "Tom knocked on the door of my apartment that night. I didn't think there was anything weird about it. He was a little drunk. So I invited him in. I thought maybe he had you out in the car or something and needed some help. Instead, he told me he had a pre-wedding gift for me. Then he pulled it out of his pants."

At this point, Nick looked horrified, saying, "His cock?"

"No, silly. The Polaroid. The one of that stripper's lips around your cock. All your friends in the background, cheering you on."

Nick at least had the decency to look ashamed.

"Oh, I was mad. And Tom was standing there with a nasty grin on his face, and I knew what would make me feel better." I paused to check on Nick. He was just sitting there, on the bed, pulling at a loose thread on his sock. I had to clear my throat to get him to make eye contact. Once he did, I continued.

"You may have noticed, but I don't like Tom. I saw him staring at my tits with that nasty grin, and I knew. . . . I knew he was there for a reason.

"He was presenting himself to me as the perfect grudge fuck, because he knows I don't like him. For me to fuck your best man before the wedding out of anger and outrage would be just the sort of thing I'd want to do after seeing that damn photo. No emotions, just angry, physical sex. He pulled a condom out of his pocket about then and if I hadn't been so pissed at you, I'd have tossed him out on his ass. So, really, what it all comes down to is it's your fault I fucked Tom."

Nick started to protest, but I wasn't about to let him off the hook so easily.

"I called him an asshole, tore up the picture, and threw the scraps in his face. Then I grabbed his package and pulled him to me. 'Hey, don't shoot the messenger,' he smirked. He might have been drunk, but he was able. I grabbed his hard cock and squeezed.

"It didn't take us long to get undressed. Turns out, he has an okay body with a great cock. It's average in length but thick with an impressive head. Just the way I like them. 'Suck me, baby,' he whispered. But I couldn't get that picture of the stripper out of my head. Instead, I sat back on the couch and spread my legs.

"He went straight to work. He licked me like he couldn't get enough. Sucking my clit into his mouth, he slipped a finger inside me. I gripped his head between my thighs and came all over his face."

I had to stop here, because Nick clearly wasn't listening to me anymore. His eyes weren't focusing well and he was sort of shaking. I thought maybe it was an allergic reaction, so I slapped him hard across the face. I don't know if that's what you do for an allergic reaction, but it felt good and he perked up a bit after that.

"So . . . to continue . . . Tom was totally ready to fuck after that. He flipped me over onto my stomach, lifted my hips so my ass was in the air, grabbed a handful of hair, and fucked me raw. I was so wet that he slid right into me.

"He fucked me hard and talked dirty. 'Take it, slut. Take that cock, whore. God, your pussy's so tight.' I was really turned on by all the heat and anger. It was wildly animalistic. I was screaming at him to fuck me hard, like a cheap whore, and he did."

Nick was quite pale by the time I got to this section of the story. I considered leaving out the rest, but I'd covered most of the juicy part already.

"It didn't last all that long. It was hot, but he was too quick. I do think he felt bad afterward. But I forgave him for not putting in the time since he'd done such a great job sucking me off earlier."

Nick sat on the bed's edge, back to me by now, slowly shaking his head. I crawled across the bed over to him and began massaging him through his shirt.

"Come on, honey." I figured it was time for some kiss-and-make-up fucking. "Let's stop talking so much and start doing what most people do on their honeymoon." With one hand, I reached around and soothed his pants' fly.

"I can't believe you fucked my best man a week before our wedding." Nick was having a hard time getting over it. "Have you been with any other guys since then?"

I thought for a moment. "No. . . . Not really. Well, not with any guys."

Nick twisted his neck around, almost like he was possessed. Who knew that a newly married man, my husband, had such flexibility? And I really didn't know he had such a vocabulary, either.

"You fucked around with a woman? When?" He slapped his hand down hard on the bed.

"This morning." I was wondering what sort of man I'd married. I mean, who talks to his new bride like that on her wedding night?

Nick placed his elbows on his thighs and buried his face in his palms.

"Who?" He whispered so softly that I could barely hear the question.

"Janice."

His shoulders slumped and his arms fell between his legs. He said, "My old girlfriend? Janice?"

"Yeah, her." I was actually glad to be getting all this out. "Remember? I told you it was a bad idea to invite your ex-girlfriend to my wedding. What were you thinking?"

Nick just sat there, dumbstruck. I guess it was all a bit much. Me not being a virgin. Me fucking his best man a week ago. Me having sex with his ex-girlfriend on our wedding day. But still, I just didn't get what he was so upset about. I didn't ever say I was a virgin. I only had sex with Tom because Nick let a stripper blow him at the bachelor party and pissed me off. And the Janice thing—well, I had told him not to invite her.

I guess all through our courtship, I had thought it was obvious that I had a lot of sexual experience. I thought he was holding off on having sex because it was some kind of fantasy he had going. I mean, granted, two years is a long-ass time to play mind games, but he got me seriously horny and worked up so that I'd have amazing, body-wrenching orgasms. And except for these last two flings, I'd not had sex with anyone in the last few months—ever since we got engaged—so I just didn't see what his problem was.

"But Janice is married! Happily married." Nick remained in denial.

"Oh, that's okay." I began to explain. "Her husband watched."

"Oh . . . my . . . God . . ." Nick's breath was erratic.

"It all started innocently enough." I tried to calm him. "It was a couple of hours before the wedding and I was in that back

room, off to the side of where we had the ceremony. I was trying to get my gown on and was having trouble with the back
zipper. I noticed that Janice and her husband had walked in. At
first, they seemed really embarrassed about it, explaining that
they'd gotten mixed up and thought it was a shortcut to the
bathrooms. Pretty funny."

"Oh, yes, really hysterical." Nick agreed—I think.

"Janice offered to leave, but I told her I needed help zipping
up. They hesitated, but then her husband, after introducing
himself, took a seat in the corner across from the mirrors, you
know?"

"No. I don't have any fucking idea." Nick exploded. "Remember, you told me it was bad luck for me to see you before
the ceremony."

"Oh, yeah. And it would have been if you'd come back when
Janice was there, I guess," I countered.

"Bad luck for whom?" he seethed.

"Well, for . . . well, I don't know. Maybe Mark."

"Mark? Who the hell is Mark?"

"Janice's husband, remember? You met him at the reception," I said incredulously. I mean really. Nick was having a
tough time keeping up.

"Why would it have been bad luck for Mark?" Nick growled.

"Why don't you let me tell you about what happened in my
own way and quit interrupting?" I snapped.

Nick seemed to realize that he was out of line and he settled
down to listen after that.

"As I was saying, Mark sat in the corner across from the mirrors." I paused here to see if there would be any more rude interruptions from my new spouse, but he just motioned for me
to keep going.

"So, I was standing before the mirror and Janice was behind

me. I stared at her dark eyes in the mirror. She stared at my reflection as she inched the zipper up my back." Here I stopped telling the story.

"You know, Nick, I can see why you liked her so much. She's hot. Pouty lips. And truly lovely breasts. And she tastes so. . . ." I had to stop because Nick choked on something, though I don't know what it could have been. When he started breathing again and the color in his face was more normal, I went back to the story.

"Where was I? Oh, right. She zipped me, but then didn't move away. She looked at me in my dress and couldn't seem to take her eyes off me. I was a little concerned that she was feeling jealous, you know, her being your ex-girlfriend and me being the woman you are about to marry, but then she just licked her lips and said, 'You're a striking woman.' A faint blush colored her cheeks as her hands drifted down to my waist. I looked into her eyes, at least into the reflection of her eyes, and I saw it. Hunger. Desire. I shivered and felt myself get wet.

"I looked away and saw her husband's reflection in the mirror. He was just staring, not blinking or moving. I thought maybe not even breathing, then I saw him take a quick breath and let it out, kind of in a shudder.

"When Jan saw my glance, she smiled. 'It's okay. He doesn't mind.'

"'Well, maybe I do,' I said to her." I looked at Nick for approval. I wanted him to see that I wasn't that easy.

He wasn't even really looking at me. He seemed off in another world. I snapped my fingers in front of his eyes and he turned to look at me like he was surprised I was there. I mean, Christ, married just a few hours and he's off daydreaming and doesn't even pay me any attention. I kept going with the story in spite of his ignoring me.

"'Have you ever been with another woman?' Janice asked me, and I said, 'Not really. I mean, I've kissed girls, but I've never gone all the way.'"

"'Don't you want to try it once? One last experiment before you tie the knot?' Her luscious smile appeared over my shoulder.

"Turning to face her, I agreed that I supposed I would be missing a golden opportunity. I figured she was right, it was best to do it before the wedding." Again, I looked to be sure Nick was getting it that I was the good girl here, just doing what was best for our marriage.

"Her hands cupped my ass, and she pulled me closer. Janice tipped my head up and kissed me. Gentle at first. Soft and slow. It was different than the sloppy, drunken kisses I'd experienced in college. Jan was a woman who knew what she was doing.

"After a few minutes, she pulled back and stared into my eyes. 'Are you wet?' And I nodded.

"'I have to taste you.' She pulled the zipper back down. 'But I don't want to ruin your beautiful dress.'

"I stepped out of the dress and watched her in the mirror as she slowly slid my panties down."

Here, I paused again. "Just to clarify, those were my other pair of wedding panties. After she got me all wet and everything, they were unwearable, so I had to use my backup thong panties. I really am sorry. I think you would have liked the first pair a lot." I was feeling a little guilty for Nick having missed that other pair, but then realized I could just wash them and wear them some other night, so I went on with my tale.

"Anyway, when I took off my bra, she bent her head and sucked my nipples. Her hot tongue moved down my body until she was kneeling before me.

"I gazed into her chocolate-colored eyes as she found my clit with her tongue. My legs trembled as she licked me all over.

Tasting me. When I couldn't stand straight anymore, I lay down on the sofa.

"'Oh, Jan.' I murmured her name as she fucked me. I remembered that you called her Jan, so it seemed right for me to call her that, too."

Here Nick put his fist up to his mouth and bit into his knuckles. I was worried that maybe I'd made a mistake marrying this man. He clearly wasn't nearly as able to control himself as I thought. God, how hard to marry someone and find out they aren't who you thought. Well, I just had to hope this was wedding night nerves or something and that he'd soon be the Nick I'd grown to love.

"She fucked me first with her tongue, then with her long, talented fingers. She fucked me with three fingers and pinched my clit with the other hand. I'm sure anyone walking outside the room could hear me screaming. When she sucked my clit into her mouth, I saw starbursts. When she was done, the seat cushion was as wet as I was.

"After she helped me put on my dress again, she gave me one last kiss. 'You were wonderful. Nick's a really lucky guy.'

"I blushed because I knew, or I guess, assumed she'd had sex with you, too.

"'Thanks!' was all I could think of to say. In a way, I *was* grateful. Jan helped me get rid of the pre-wedding jitters."

Nick stood up and slowly paced the room.

"There hasn't been anyone else since her, Nick." I thought that might help. Oops. I was forgetting. "Unless you count a hand job. But it was just a little one."

Nick stopped pacing and stared at me. I guess he didn't dare ask.

"Mark. You do remember Mark, don't you?" I demanded,

thinking if he couldn't follow this, I'd made a huge mistake in marrying him.

"He was all, you know, aroused, so I figured it was the polite thing to do, me being the hostess and all."

Nick turned completely away from me. I was sure this marriage was over and I hadn't even digested the wedding cake yet. I guess I'd have to give back the ring. And all the gifts. I wondered how I might spend these couple weeks off from work without a husband.

Just as I was starting to come up with some ideas of what I'd do at the resort all alone on my non-honeymoon, Nick surprised me by letting out a little half laugh. He still wouldn't turn to look at me, so I moved over to him and ran my fingers along his ass.

"You know, Nick, I really do only love you." I thought it was obvious, but maybe he had to actually hear it.

When I finally dared to peek around his side, his face didn't look angry anymore. And when I reached around and touched his hardening cock, I knew we'd weathered our first fight as husband and wife. He was ready for me, the real me. Not the woman he'd pretended I was.

It wasn't too long after that before I had his clothes off again and he'd replaced his pout with a grin.

We fucked for hours. Woke up the next morning and fucked again. I guess my past didn't matter as much to Nick as he thought it would. Probably because a smart man would rather be jealous of a slut than bored by a saint.

Francis Underwood

Great story with twists and turns. Think The Thomas Crown Affair *with an edge.*

Screwed Over ... and Over

He certainly wasn't hard to recognize. He looked absolutely dapper as he examined one of the gallery's paintings. A glass of white wine cradled between two fingers added to the image. His crisp blue suit was tailored to show off his every move. He had sun-baked skin, deep and even, and his beard was trimmed neat and clean, as clean and crisp as everything about him.

His shadow was there, too. The bodyguard who never had to blink and was never more than a few yards away.

My heels clicked across the stone floor while my black silk gown, sides slit, drifted with me. I stopped at his side so we could share the painting, just as planned. To me it looked like it was created by a blind man throwing paint-covered baseballs at a carny, trying desperately to hit anything in order to win a big stuffed doggy. Maybe worse.

"What crap," I said to get his attention.

"Crap?" He cocked his head. A long pause, then, "Yes. I guess it is. Crap."

I laughed and he introduced himself as Paul.

"Nicole," was the name I gave him as a few of my fingertips touched the top of his right hand.

It was all flirts and laughs for the hours after that. We started with a couple of espressos at an outdoor bistro followed by a slow walk along the river to a pretentious little restaurant—pretentious and Pakistani. He topped our sudden date off with a fast kiss on the slow elevator ride up to his suite.

Paul DeBasse was very predictable. He always flew into town the third week of the month on a Tuesday and stayed for just under seventy-two hours. He didn't do this every month, just seven out of twelve. The Wednesday afternoon after he arrived, he checked out a gallery, then a bistro, then had an ethnic dinner somewhere along the river. He rarely left a gallery alone, but was always looking for company. He didn't have to look very hard, even with his burly babysitter never far away. It was a little strange, having this goon follow us about. I wondered what all the other women must think, but then stopped worrying about them and started focusing on my job: Paul. Paul always returned to his hotel by nine P.M. and within eight hours he was back on his private jet.

I doubted that all art thieves were as predictable.

His people prowled the world for art: spoils of war, stolen antiques, and even good forgeries. He never touched the stuff himself, only the money. Well, he touched the money and he touched me, too.

He was all manners and class until that suite's door closed the world outside, leaving his bodyguard in the hall. Then, he was just another guy with octopus arms, a fast tongue, and little imagination. Of course, I wasn't there to enjoy myself, so it didn't particularly matter if he was about as erotic as a mud puddle with no concept of foreplay.

"Go easy, baby." My tongue pushed the words into his ear, but he wasn't listening. All that blood rushing from his brain to his cock must have been deafening. He grabbed my gown straps and tugged them down my shoulders to expose my lacy bra. Then he tried to tug that off, too.

"Hold on." My palms pushed his chest and I stepped back to

unhook the clasp and let it fall on its own. The sight of my breasts riled him up. As he took two steps toward me, I took three steps back, until I was pressed against the bathroom door.

"Paul? A bedroom?" I was no lady, but I'm no whore either. My ice-water words stunned him momentarily, then he recovered.

"Of course." He backed away, then led me to the bed. It was a passing respite because no sooner was I beginning to get comfortable then he was at me again, shoving me onto my back, twisting and stretching my gown until it dangled off one ankle. He wasn't nearly so polite with my panties, which came off in two pieces, maybe three.

His face pushed my thighs apart and his lips gripped my pussy like a suction cup. His tongue behaved like a paintbrush making pop art and his hands grabbed my ass, stuffing his pinkies in my crack. He sure was making me wet . . . with his own spit. However he managed it, he did get one little orgasm out of me, though I'd chalk that up to a freak accident rather than talent.

Basically, his lovemaking, like the painting, was crap in my book.

I relaxed while he finally removed his own clothes, carefully hanging up his suit and neatly folding his shirt, shorts, and even his socks. He was a righteous prick and a prissy one at that. However, it turned out he possessed a mighty prick as well.

His cock was longer than most I'd known, and though I've seen my share, its head could have passed for a doorknob.

Soon he was on me again, licking my face as aimlessly as he'd licked me below and slipping his cock in and out of me. I hated admitting this, but his cock was hitting spots in me that were pushing me over the edge. His fucking was like a blind man throwing hard baseballs . . . you get where I'm going. Pretending he was a vibrator, I came a couple more times before he shuddered and came inside me.

Collapsing on top of me with all his weight, he was, I realized, announcing that he was done. That was fine with me. I, however, was not done. Teasing his balls with my fingertips, I prodded his cock back to life, then climbed aboard for a nice long ride. I rode him to exhaustion and on to the edge of death's bed. I rode him until I forgot his name, forgot my own name, forgot just about everything. Everything but the job, that is. That stayed right there in the back of my mind, niggling and tickling and keeping me from losing it all. We came together the second time with my orgasm drowning out his.

As I said, I forgot everything but the job. Just as I came, the second hand ticked the final second of 9:39 and I was off him and on my way. Claiming a need to wee, I pretended to hit the head only to dodge to the front door. Before 9:40 ticked its way past, I opened the door, shocking the unshockable bodyguard as he eyed me in my altogether, distracting him long enough for my partner to pop out from the adjacent stairwell and pop him one on the back of his head. Marvin's a sap for a sap, and for this gig he used a sock full of quarters. I worried a bit that the bodyguard's head wasn't hard enough, but saw him breathing sweetly in his sudden sleep and let it pass.

We'd planned this out for months. We could never be sure of when DeBasse was in town, what hotel he'd stay in, what bistro or restaurant he'd visit. But we could guess which gallery. We staked out the one we were betting on each Wednesday afternoon and it wasn't long before we got the big payout. With luck like ours, I was planning on hitting Vegas. Each Wednesday, I would ready myself for Mr. DeBasse. I'd paint my toenails, shave my legs, brush and floss, then slip into the little slip of a slinky black dress. I also practiced describing every painting I saw as "crap."

My partner went on to take care of DeBasse while I dragged the guard's body inside the room. When I saw DeBasse again he was on the floor, eyes shut and blood trickling out of his nose.

Ah, well. Fuck him.

My partner and I began searching under the bed, the closets, the luggage, and even inside the pillows and mattress. Our planning and scheming were turning into a bad investment. Marvin had more money in his spare sock than we were finding in that suite. I bummed a smoke from my partner and stepped out on the balcony for a quick one. That's where I found the black bag tucked in a corner. It was a beautifully simple spot, right out in the open air. And inside was about ten times the cash we'd hoped for.

Going down in the elevator, the bag's strap crossing my shoulder, I glanced at Marvin.

"I parked in back. Looked safer."

"Okay. Sure." Off plan, but it was no problem for me. His job was to scope out the hotel. Mine was to get laid.

I led him through the rear exit. Once among the smell of Dumpsters and rancid water puddles, I heard a clink. Then I felt that sock full of quarter rolls across the back of my head.

I woke up later surrounded by plastic bags full of trash. Left for dead, all I had were my clothes, a stench in my nose, and a headache that Houdini couldn't have escaped from.

I was a dumb, fucking broad. I had figured that being a broad willing to fuck, dumb as that may be, was worth half a fortune in free cash.

Marvin apparently disagreed and wanted it all.

Two Months Later . . .

When I entered the bedroom, the first thing I saw was Marvin's bare ass, pale but tight enough to smack. His ass bobbed up and down like he was in a contest for the quickest fuck. I couldn't see the chick, just her two legs high up in the air. Her yelps were loud but fake. A woman always knows these things.

I stood in the doorway, my equipment bag over my shoulder, unnoticed. His date was making such a commotion neither of them heard me sneak in. No matter how many times I had told him, Marvin never did invest in a real security system but had continued to rely upon just a few shoddy locks that I could pick in minutes.

Her moans hit a higher pitch and his sad, bony ass moved lightning quick. Just as his butt clenched for one last thrust, I stomped in and said, "Hey, Marvin."

He screamed and got off her, scooting across the mattress like a crab, his cock spurting come all over the surprised chick.

"What the hell?" she shouted. She wiped away the few drops that splattered on her neck. I had time to look her over and appreciated her shapely hips and expensive-looking chest. She was completely shaved below except for a neatly trimmed patch right above her pink clit, letting me know Marvin had found himself a natural redhead.

"Charlene, what a surprise!" Marvin's voice was casual, calm, and even, as though we were two old friends who happened to bump into one other on the street.

"Long time no see," I said. I made a point of staring at his shrinking dick. It was barely a mouthful, even mostly erect. No wonder his lady friend looked bored.

"Where have you been hiding? I was so worried about you," he said.

I resisted the urge to knock the smile off his face. I bet he was worried. Worried that the sock full of quarters he'd slapped across the back of my head might have left a mark. It probably did.

I walked closer to the bed, giving him a good look at what was tucked in my waistband. His eyes grew wide. He had never seen me become violent. Then again, I never thought my partner—I mean, ex-partner—would ever try to betray me.

He put his hands up. "The money's under the bed, darling. Take what you want and leave."

"Not going to fall for that one," I said. Marvin continued to sit near the headboard, his legs tucked close to his chest. I motioned for the redhead to get off the bed.

"Are you going to be a problem?" I asked her.

"No," she whispered. She glanced at Marvin, then leaned close to me. "The bag's in the closet."

Marvin lunged toward her. "You fucking whore!"

"Sit down," I told him, touching the butt of my piece to his head for emphasis. He sat still, his eyes locked on the redhead, his hand rubbing the little sore spot on his head. Fuck him. Couldn't hurt nearly as bad as a sock full of coins.

The duffel bag was right where the charming redhead had said. The idiot didn't even bother to hide it. I unzipped it, breathing in the smell of new money. It had been the perfect score and looked like Marvin hadn't dipped into it too much over the past two months.

Marvin remained crouched in the same position. He looked tired, defeated. "Are you taking all of it?" he asked me.

I didn't answer. Once it might have been fair to just take half. That was before he tried to shut my eyes permanently. I tossed a piece of nylon rope to the chick. She caught it, not knowing what to do with it.

"Marvin, lie facedown on the floor." Turning toward the girl, I said, "Tie his hands behind his back. Then his ankles."

She was quick to follow directions, which I instantly liked about her. When she was done, she came back toward me; her wide eyes looked me up and down, clearly waiting for my next instruction. I didn't exactly trust those doe eyes of hers, and knew it was an act to stay on my good side, but then again, I wanted her. Wanted her enough to figure she wasn't really on

Marvin's team or she'd have put up more of a fight. Anyway, with his little package, I figured her for a rental since no woman I know would tie herself down with Marvin for free. I set my gun on the nightstand.

She was an average kisser, held back by her nerves. I guessed it for her first time with another woman. She let me lead, and that was fine by me. I cupped her tits, pressed them together and ran my tongue between them, licking her nipples until they were hard. I dipped my fingers into her, enjoying her smooth skin.

"What's going on?" Marvin said. I don't like interruptions, so I kicked him. It felt almost as good as her soft, wet folds. After I undressed, I shoved my panties into his mouth.

I never asked the redhead's name. Didn't need to know anything about her. Spreading her thighs, I massaged her clit with my thumb and wanted to taste her, but not after Marvin had been there. I can't do sloppy seconds.

So I did the next best thing. I straddled her face, pressed myself against her mouth. Gently at first, but as she licked me with a tentative tongue, I grew more aggressive.

"That's it, baby," I purred. "Taste my pussy."

Her tongue moved to my clit, flicking it, teasing. I pressed between her lips, softly grinding against her. When I came, she licked me all over. I returned the favor and cleaned her face with my tongue.

Slipping my fingers down, I discovered she was soaking wet. I easily slid two fingers inside her. I wouldn't use my mouth on her, but I had other tricks and I showed them to her, teaching her how deft my fingers could be, better than any vibrator. By the time she stopped shaking, I was already dressed. Ready to take what was mine and head to Vegas. Kind of cliché, but a cliché is a cliché because it's true.

Thinking back, I should have known something was wrong.

She was too easy, too willing to spread her legs for me. Stupid me, I thought I convinced her with my sex appeal.

"Don't move."

Just two words, and I recognized that voice. I didn't even need to turn around, but I did. The redhead was just a prop. She had stalled while waiting for Paul DeBasse. He'd had the same two months to track down Marvin, but now that I think about it, he probably tracked me down, since he hadn't seen Marvin and I wasn't hiding much since I didn't have the cash. Fuck. That was *truly* stupid on my part. He just waited for me to find Marvin, then set him up with the redhead. I just happened to choose the same time and day for my attack, making it a perfect trifecta.

I thought of making a suicide play by going for my piece, but I'd left it on the nightstand. Now the redhead was twirling it around her index finger like in a black-and-white western.

"Nice to see you again, Paul," I smiled. I had nothing better.

"Nicole." He tipped his forehead.

"Her name's Charlene." The redhead had become annoying. She talked too fucking much.

With the intros out of the way, DeBasse took his money and his redhead back. He charged me some interest, too—a hard tap on my still-sore head.

I woke up a while later, sharing the floor with Marvin. He was still tied up and chewing on my panties. He was making a lot of noise and I bet he was demanding that I let him loose.

I didn't. I left my ex-partner like that. With any luck, some-one would find him in a few days. Hopefully, his mother.

Then I headed to Vegas for a night of booze and strippers. I still had a pocket full of credit cards. There was no sense in drop-ping a good plan just because of a headache.

Oni Nurani

JennaTip #3: Girl-on-Girl Experimentation

YES!

Oh. You want something more than wholehearted support? Okay.

There is absolutely nothing wrong with wanting to sample the cookies. You're not alone in fantasizing about it or trying it or loving it.

Before going for it, though, be sure you are upfront about this being new and that you are just trying it out, if that's where you are. This way you can avoid misunderstandings, and no one gets hurt. It's okay to just want to play, but be sure you're both on the same page. This goes for sex with anyone. If you don't know if you could be serious or not, then be honest about that, too.

Are you experimenting because you just want to see what the big deal is, or because you've always been interested and attracted to other women, or because it's the "thing" to do? Before you do anything, figure out your motivation.

Some women have sex with other women to explore and discover their sexuality. Afterward you may decide you prefer girls or prefer guys or don't have a preference but love them both! Sex and love come in all sorts of flavors, so get out there and start tasting!

It Will All End in Tears

I leaned low over the table, almost spilling my breasts from the low-cut neckline of my dress. My four friends ogled me.

Scarlet, shapely and with naturally wavy red hair, licked her lips, ending with the tip of her pink tongue withdrawing slowly back into her mouth at the far left corner. "You look good enough to eat, Diana."

Giving her a smoldering look, I said, "Funny, but that's exactly what Rick tells me . . . every night."

"You horny slut!" Scarlet said with a deadpan smirk.

"Funny again—that's what Rick calls *you*.'"

"He never does!"

"That's what he called you on Thursday, wasn't it? You didn't object then."

"Thursday?" Scarlet flushed deeply up her alabaster neck, matching her skin to her name.

I lifted an eyebrow. "That's right, Thursday. I was supposed to be back late but I got home early. You were on your knees, lovely lips around his hard cock. I remember perfectly. He bellowed, 'You horny slut!' just as he grasped that fabulous hair in his fist and slammed his dick to the back of your throat. Or at least that's the way it looked to me from my position."

"I—I—" Scarlet lapsed into silence.

After a somewhat uncomfortable pause, Mina, with her milk-chocolate skin and feral look, spat, "Men!" She took a long, deep sip of her drink, dabbing delicately at her lips with her napkin as though washing out her mouth and cleaning off something a bit dirty.

Her lover, Veronica, closed her almond eyes, covering Mina's hand with her own. "What do you expect from a man, Diana dear?"

"Girls don't cheat on girls?" I asked.

"No."

"But you have."

Veronica sat back. Mina turned to look at her, then turning to me, said, "Not while she's been with me!"

I said, "Don't act so shocked, Mina. I know you've cheated, too!"

"All of you are cheats. Cheats and sluts. Every last one of you has been with my Rick."

"What are you getting at?" Hannah, voluptuous and forty, demanded.

I smiled. "Scarlet's fucked my Rick behind my back. So have you, Hannah, and you two as well—not only have you all fucked my man but you've all cheated on each other. You're all sluts!"

Mina and Veronica glared at each other. Hannah kept her face blank. Scarlet grinned. "So, Diana," she drawled, "your boy toy has been cheating on you with all of us, and on each of us with the rest of us. What do you think of that?"

"What do I think? I think that you should each have asked permission to play with my toy and not just taken my plaything without asking. Didn't your mothers ever teach you any manners at all? I know my mother did. She also taught me about sharing."

The girls were all astounded.

"Girls. . . . men are just men. They don't provide the support and love that women do. Did you all really think that I'd let a man, no matter how talented, come between us? Never. However, while I am ready to forgive you, each and every one, I do think we should teach that double-crossing bastard a lesson."

"Like?" Mina asked.

"Cut him off," Veronica suggested. "We should swear never to fuck Rick again!"

I said, "Right, and what then? Knowing my Rick, he'd find another girl in a week and be cheating on her within a month."

Hannah mused, "He's a damned good fuck. We mustn't forget that."

"Then?" Veronica asked.

I leaned forward. "The bastard thinks he's some sort of super-stud."

"Isn't he?" Scarlet put in.

I said, "Not as super as he thinks he is. I think we should teach him a real lesson. What if we . . ."

My friends huddled together as I explained my plan.

Rick had turned our second bedroom into a home gym. I was all for it. I like it that he keeps in shape, plus I work out three times a week myself. Then there was sex on the incline bench or with me hanging from the chinning bar. Exercise equipment can be fun.

The Sunday afternoon after my meeting with my friends, I walked in on Rick when he was on his back, pressing a hefty barbell. My cropped T-shirt was just long enough to cover my nipples. Instead of my usual shorts, I wore lacy little wide-legged panties that were cut low enough that my pubic hair would have shown above them if I hadn't shaved baby-smooth.

Rick's eyes widened. I looked him up and down, bulging biceps, sweat-slick chest, and old rugger pants. I licked my lips.

The barbell clanged into its rack. Rick began to sit up.

"Don't stop," I said. "Watching you work out turns me on."

"Does it?" He took a grip on the bar and began pressing it again.

I smoothed my palm down his chest, savoring the way his pecs rippled as he pumped iron.

"Twenty-seven," he grunted.

My fingers found the elastic of his pants, three inches below his navel. "Keep going."

"Twenty-eight."

"Can you do fifty? I'll give you a special treat if you can do fifty."

"Oh? Twenty . . . nine."

"Something really special," I promised. I began to drag his pants lower.

Rick managed to heave his butt up off the bench. I tugged his pants from beneath him and all the way off.

"You look so good in just that tiny jockstrap," I told him, stroking his inner thigh.

"Thirty! I'm gonna burst right out of it if you keep that up."

My fingertips trailed over the cotton that was being stretched by his cock. "Do fifty for me, baby!"

"Thirty-one."

My finger worked under his jock and found hot skin. "*Now* you're pumping iron." That was our signal. My friends crept in behind Rick.

Each had prepared in her own way. Hannah was naked except for high heels, black hose, a waspie, and a choker. She was carrying a small purse. Scarlet had a towel around her hips and nothing else. Mina was simply bare, with a vibrator clenched in her fist. Veronica, playing on her Chinese looks, wore a vivid red cheongsam with a slit up between her legs, exposing her bald pussy; she also carried a vibrator—a longer and thinner one, with a kink at the end. Each of them clutched a roll of duct tape with one end dangling.

I straddled Rick's muscular thighs, leaned forward, and pressed down on his chest.

He grunted, "Forty!"

"Ten to go!"

"Do I smell perfume?" Rick asked.

"It's new," I explained. "Don't stop, Rick!"

My four friends kept quiet as Rick strained through the rest of the set. At forty-nine his arms were trembling. Halfway though fifty he paused, gathered his strength, and heaved. His bar clanged into the rack.

"Now!" I repeated.

Moving with deft speed, Hannah and Scarlet wrapped Rick's wrists with duct tape, then over the bar and round the rack.

"What?" Rick bellowed.

Mina and Veronica threw themselves at Rick's ankles and started taping them. Rick squirmed and heaved. "What do you—?"

Hannah and Scarlet joined me and the other two. Between us, we fought Rick's flailing legs and heaved him down the bench until his tailbone was perched on the very edge. Secured like that, arms stretched up and back, legs bent under him and taped at the ankles to the bench's legs, Rick was helpless and very vulnerable.

"Is this some sort of joke?" he demanded.

"It's time to teach you a little lesson, lover," I cooed.

"What sort of . . . ? Oh, no!" His eyes were riveted to the oversized pair of shears that I was brandishing. "What are you doing?" he screeched.

"You'll see." I worked one blade between the cup of his jockstrap and his tightening balls.

"No!"

I snipped. The jockstrap parted. Rick's balls burst free to dangle between his spread thighs.

Snip! The waistband parted. I snatched the ruined garment away. Rick's cock quivered. It half rose, then subsided, then rose again, confused. Being surrounded by five mostly naked women excited it. The shears scared it.

I laid the shears aside. Reassured, Rick's cock rose again, high and proud, thickening as it lengthened.

"I can dig it," Rick said.

"Can you, lover?" I asked. "We'll see."

"If you want me to fuck you all, fine by me, but this isn't the best position . . ."

"No!" I interrupted. "You've got it wrong, Rick. You aren't going to fuck us. We are going to fuck you!"

Hannah knelt between Rick's thighs. "I love cock," she gloated.

"Aren't you forgetting something?" Scarlet asked. "He has to last like he's never lasted before, right?"

"I haven't forgotten," the older woman purred. She pulled an arrangement of leather straps from her purse.

Rick groaned as her expert fingers tugged his left ball through a loop, then his right. Thongs were tied around the base of his straining cock. Hannah was very careful to position the knot exactly right. "Wait till you get to rub your clits on this," she explained. "It's so special!" Her finger and thumb found a strip of leather that hung below Rick's balls. She pulled. The restraints tightened.

"Careful!" Rick shouted.

Hannah tugged harder. Leather bit into the base of Rick's cock, strangling it. His balls bulged until their skin was glossy.

"What's the big idea?" he demanded.

"We'll let you come, Rick," Scarlet explained, "but not until we're ready . . . and it won't come easy. Hannah says that when a guy's balls and cock are tied up like this it can take hours."

"I can go for hours," he boasted.

"Yes, you can," I said, "but with five girls playing with you at once? Maybe. Maybe not. We don't plan on taking any chances."

Hannah sat back on her haunches and took a handful of lipsticks from her purse. She tossed one, each a different color, to each of us.

I explained as they all slathered their lips. "You've fantasized about this idea of girls getting together to have a 'rainbow' party, Rick. Well, I always thought it a bit juvenile of you and imagined that it was only an urban myth. However, once the girls and I came up with this little lesson plan for you, it seemed the perfect start. Are you prepared?"

Hannah "mmm'd" her lips.

"Sure."

Her lush mouth opened wide. She took hold of Rick's rigid cock and dragged it up from where it'd been flat on his belly. She steered his stiffy into her waiting mouth. Her lips closed, just below its bulbous weeping head.

"Oh yeah!" Rick sighed.

Hannah's lips worked, smearing a ring of lipstick around the full girth of his cock. "There," she said as she drew back. "I've left lots of room."

"Me next," Veronica insisted. "I haven't had the practice at this that you lot have." She took Hannah's place and parted her lips. Her mouth was the smallest of the five. Where Hannah had simply opened wide and engulfed Rick's purple plum, Veronica had to work at stretching her lips over it.

"Oh fuck! That feels so good," Rick moaned.

Her tiny mouth fitted tightly just below the mark that Hannah had made. To be sure she'd leave a complete ring, she twisted from side to side. Rick's hips jerked. I pushed down on his pubes.

"That's cheating," I warned.

"The things she's doing with her tongue!" Rick gasped.

"Are you licking?" Mina demanded of her lesbian lover.

Veronica shrugged and plopped her mouth off. "You can go next."

Mina didn't go straight for Rick's aching cock. With a wink to Scarlet, she extended her serpentine tongue to its fullest. Its tip circled Rick's left testicle, then his right.

"Oh fuck, suck me, you bitch!" he moaned.

"There's no rush," I told him. "How about I give you something nice to look at?" My thumbs pushed my panties down. I put a foot beside him and stepped up. I perched my bottom in the middle of the bar he was taped to, so that my cunt was exposed just above his face. My fingers spread its lips wide, giving my victim a clear view of the mottled pink, soaking wet inside. "Anyone want a taste of this?" I asked.

"Me!" Hannah volunteered. The harlot straddled Rick's chest, making sure to spread her own cunt on his bare skin. Her tongue stretched out. She leaned forward and slurped me from base to clit. "Delicious," she exclaimed. "Want some tit, Rick?" She pulled his head up and fed him an engorged nipple.

Rick slobbered and his cheeks hollowed but his eyes were strained up, engrossed by the sight of Hannah's expert tongue-fucking of my cunt.

Mina moved from Rick's balls to the base of his cock. The tip of her tongue vibrated as she made a high-pitched trilling sound. Inch by slow inch, it crept higher, working its way up his shaft toward his throbbing knob.

Veronica said, "I go crazy when she does that on my clit!"

Hannah hollowed her back to force more of her breast into Rick's mouth. "Chew on it, Rick! Make it hurt good!" She reached behind herself with both hands and spread the plump cheeks of her bum. Between gobbles at my cunt, she gasped, "Someone do my ass!"

Scarlet allowed her towel to fall to the floor. "How about this?" She turned the base of the long thin vibrator with a kinked end.

"No," I interrupted. "I'm sure that Hannah loves it when Rick buggers her, don't you Hannah?"

She nodded, dragging the flat of her tongue over my clit.

"You do the honors, Scarlet." I gave her a wink.

She squeezed a dollop of Sta-Hard into her palm. It's a topical analgesic for men who come too quickly. The lotion, along with the three crushed Viagra pills I'd added to his lunchtime chili, plus the cock bondage, made up most of my magic spell. There was just one thing more.

Hannah squidged down Rick's body, depriving him of her tit and me of her tongue. Mina spread Hannah's cheeks. Scarlet guided Rick's cock. Hannah sat down with a contented sigh, impaling herself.

"Keep still," I commanded.

Scarlet knew what to do. She lubed the long thin vibrator and touched its tip to the pucker of Rick's bum.

His eyes opened wide. "No! I don't do that!"

"You don't have to do anything," I said, and nodded at Scarlet.

She pushed, slowly but firmly, working the vibe up Rick's rectum.

"You fucking bitches!" he protested, and was ignored. Then it got worse for him. Scarlet had to press the kink in the cylinder onto Rick's prostate. The only way she could be sure she was doing that was by working a finger in beside the dildo. My poor darling squirmed and swore and threatened. Scarlet switched on. Rick's eyes bulged. As if in a trance, he humped up as best he could against his restraints. Hannah squirmed happily. Scarlet wrapped her free arm around Hannah to toy with her clit. Mina, not wanting to be left out, diddled me, leaving Veronica to finger Scarlet from behind. We all squealed and moaned and groaned, partly because it came naturally and partly to increase Rick's excitement. I came first. My fingers spread my cunt's lips. I squatted over Rick's face so he could suck the juices from me.

Hannah was next. When she lifted off Rick's cock it was bigger and stiffer than I'd ever seen it, and deep purple. Two of my friends attacked it at once. Mina stroked it with both hands while Veronica opened her mouth wide an inch beyond its head.

"Give it to me, Rick," she demanded. "Come in my mouth! Let me taste your hot cream!"

Rick groaned into my pussy, "I'm trying to, you bitch! I'm trying!"

Hannah and I stood to each side of his head, reaching over him to diddle each other. Mina mounted him, facing his feet, and took over the thin vibrator from Scarlet, freeing her to use the thick one on herself, all the while giving Rick a commentary on what it felt like. Mina came on Rick's cock and was replaced by Veronica, squatting and gyrating her hips.

I held Rick's hair, forcing him to turn to watch as I ate Hannah out. I think it was Scarlet who was first to stick her come-smeared fingers into Rick's mouth. It seemed like a good idea, so we all did it each time we came or when someone else came on our fingers. Hannah went one better. When I came into her mouth—and I come very wet—she passed my juices on to Rick with a big sloppy kiss.

After a couple of hours all of us women had come at least three times. Poor Rick was in an agonizing delirium of lust. His cock was a gnarly, throbbing club. His eyes were glazed and he might have been drooling. It was hard to tell with all the girl-come on his face. His eyes rolled up. I threw a basin of icy water over him.

He spluttered back to his senses. "Please, Diana? Let me? I gotta! Have mercy."

I said, "Hannah, get ready." I wiped the Sta-Hard off his cock and replaced it with regular sex lube. The girls gathered round to watch. Scarlet tickled his bum hole. Veronica fed him a nipple. I worked his cock, two-handed. His bum lifted up off the bench despite the duct tape.

I said, "Now!"

Hannah loosed the bow she'd tied around his equipment. He let out a mighty sigh. Three more quick strokes released the most spectacular fountain of jism I'd ever seen.

He lay there, panting. At last he managed to ask, "Are you going to release me now?"

I gave him a wicked grin. "Oh no. Hannah's going to tie you up again. We're going to start over."

He looked horrified. "Please, no. Diana, I promise, I'll never cheat on you again. Please, please—no more. I'll be faithful."

"But that's not what I want," I said.

"No?"

"From now on, Rick, you are our sex slave—all of us. We won't have to worry about you cheating because by the time you've serviced all five of us, maybe two or three a day, or even at one time, you won't have anything left for other women."

You'd think a man would be delighted to be told he was at the disposal of a sexy harem, but Rick just burst into tears.

Ty Nirav

JennaTip #4: S & M—Cock and Ball Torture

Now, granted the women in that story were trying to teach him a lesson, but cock rings and cock bondage can definitely be used for pleasure. If you want to prolong his hard-on and don't want to use Viagra and don't like the numbing lubes (they'll numb you, too), then a nice cock ring will work wonders. Just don't make it super tight. It should fit a little loose around his cock and balls when he's not hard so that his dick has room to expand.

You can buy a cock ring just about anywhere. They're sold with condoms at drugstores nowadays. To use most of them, put his balls through the ring one at a time then slip his soft cock through. A few just require you to put the cock through, but that's the minority.

If the ring is too tight, don't leave it on. The problem is that he may not be able to get soft once hard, so you need to be able to get the ring off, with safety scissors if you have to. That's a problem with a metal cock ring that won't stretch. It not only has no give, but you can't cut it off either.

You can try a leather contraption like in the story. It is adjustable, so if it's too loose or too tight, it's easy to tug a little here and there to make it fit.

You can do permanent damage with cock rings and such, so be careful. If there is visible swelling of the soft layer of the cock and balls right near or under the cock ring or straps, loosen immediately. That's a sign that the circulation is cut off. You do not want to do that. You can end up losing the penis, causing nerve damage, and so on. That's not fun for anyone.

Basically, loosen the binding every twenty to thirty minutes and let the blood flow whether you think there's a problem or not. That's safest.

Two Balls and One Stroke

Every light I hit was a red one. Drove down the wrong street and had to backtrack. Then I hit a dead end and needed a seven-point turn to change course. Why did this always happen when I was in a rush? If I didn't find this place soon, and get back home soon after that, I'd miss the big game.

Finally pulled into a small parking lot with more dirt than pavement. The building looked smaller than I expected. Wasn't sure I was in the right place. No sign at the door. I walked inside and spotted the young receptionist. Asian, petite, could have been pretty except for the diamond stud on her left nostril. Never understood why girls mutilate themselves.

I stood there, waiting for her to look up. I cleared my throat. "Excuse me. Do you speak English?"

She rolled her eyes. "Yeah. Do you?"

"Oh, sorry." She didn't even have an accent. "Am I at the right place?"

"Depends," she said. "What're you looking for?"

She wasn't making this easy for me. I took the wrinkled business card out of my pocket. It barely survived a wash, but the street address was semilegible. "Is this where I can get a massage?"

She smirked. "Sure. If that's what you're looking for."

What was that supposed to mean? "Well, I got this referral for some kind of special treatment?"

"The special treatment? We get referrals for that all the time. We got the best hands in the county."

I rubbed my lower back. The long drive had made the pain even worse. "So can I book a treatment today?"

"Sure. Just fill this out, and Nicki will be with you in Room J."

I took the form and gave her my credit card. She took it, looked at me a little strangely, then processed it.

"People usually pay cash here."

I didn't know what to say to that. Seemed odd. But I'd never been to a place like this before, so what did I know?

She handed me a fluffy white towel and pointed down the hallway toward the locker rooms. Then she went back to looking bored.

The facilities were modern. Everything white and immaculate. I grabbed a quick shower and took a clean robe from a stack. Then I headed down another corridor. Only saw one other person. Some skinny guy who wouldn't look me in the eyes. I expected a bigger crowd, people walking around. Jocks spanking each other with towels. This was supposed to be the best spa on the West Coast.

Ronnie, my agent, recommended this place. All the top athletes came here to unwind, soothe their battered muscles. It had been a while since I was at the pro level. It's been years since I touched a baseball. But my body was still recovering.

When my back started bugging me, Ronnie pushed me to book an appointment. "I guarantee you'll love it."

"I don't know," I told him. "Ain't into that metrosexual hogwash. I don't want any hippie rubbing me up with smelly oil."

"Trust me," he said. "If it's good enough for a Hall of Famer, it's good enough for you."

Point taken.

I soon found Room J. My storage shed was bigger. There weren't any wall decorations or charts. Floor was bare. Nothing in the room but a chair and a massage table. Was I supposed to wait for my masseuse? Or should I lie down on the table first? I just wished she'd hurry. I had a hundred riding on the big game and didn't want to miss a second of it.

I jumped when the door opened. Turned around and saw a pixie of a woman. She was barely five feet tall, lean frame. No, maybe tiny is a better word. Fair skin with straight black hair that hung all the way down to her lower back. She was dressed simply in a white top and thin shorts. Like something a woman would wear while watching television in bed.

"Hi, I'm Nicki." She shook my hand with a strong grip.

"Nice to meet you." I pointed at the table. "Should I get on top?"

"That's the way it usually works," she laughed, a glint of metal sparkling inside her mouth. A tongue piercing. I wondered if all the girls here had piercings. Seemed unprofessional for an upscale place. Of course, everything so far was a surprise and very different from what I expected.

I took off the robe and climbed onto the table, facedown and wearing nothing but a watch. I was skeptical. To my eyes, she looked a bit small to be a masseuse. She had strong hands, but I needed some real deep-tissue work.

"So, what are you looking for today?" she asked as she rubbed her hands together fast, like she was going to start a fire or something.

"I have lower back pain due to some injuries. A friend told me the special treatment would help loosen me up."

"I guarantee the special treatment will totally loosen you up," she said, but then I swear she muttered under her breath, "and it might even help your back pain."

Not sure of what I'd heard, I pushed to get us down to business.

"How long is this going to take?"

Before I could say anything else, she got to work on my sore muscles. Starting with my shoulders, her fingers and palms attacked my flesh. I closed my eyes and tried to enjoy it. But not too much. I was known to get a hard-on when an attractive woman washed and cut my hair. And this was a lot more personal and harder to hide. I opened my eyes again when she stopped. Then felt some warm oil being drizzled on my shoulders and back.

"You're Benny. Benny Dugan, right?" she asked. Crap. It was a bad time to be thinking of autographs.

"That's me." I kept it simple.

She was pressing on me again, just below the shoulders, using the heels of her palms to dig deep. At times it hurt so much that it made me shudder. But mostly it felt so good I wanted it to last forever.

"I remember you pitching that game against the Cubs," she started again. "The one-hitter. Beautiful." She added a soft whistle.

"Thanks."

"Too bad about the injury." She was talking about the ball that hit me in the wrist and pretty much ended my career.

More oil, now onto my lower back. This is the area that had been bothering me lately. Felt like a twisted-up garden hose. I'd have sworn she had a dozen hands working on me. Pressing, kneading, pushing. It all felt great, but temporary. I knew that when she stopped, the pain would return.

"I miss seeing your butt on the field." She giggled for a second, then stopped with a fake cough. That was the nickname my female fans had given me: Benny the Butt, best backside in baseball. It was even featured once on the cover of a major sports magazine.

Then Nicki did the weirdest thing. She poured oil all over my ass and upper thighs. My back arched as the grease worked into my crack and down to my balls. I turned my head toward her and saw that she was doing another weird thing—taking off her shirt.

She dropped the shirt to the floor and stood there proudly baring her chest. Her breasts were small with peaked nipples. I wanted to reach over and touch her, but figured that was one sure way of being tossed out of that place. It was okay, though. She did it for me. Took some of my oil and rubbed it onto her breasts and cleavage.

I kept the vision of her shining breasts and thin waist in my mind as my eyes closed. Her skilled fingers began rubbing my ass cheeks and upper legs. When she prodded for me to spread my thighs apart, I did. As she worked my inseam, her fingers gently brushed my balls. Accidentally, I thought. Still, the touch woke up my cock and it began to harden and grow.

I might have been embarrassed if she hadn't, as suddenly and this time absolutely deliberately, grabbed onto my balls with one hand as the fingers of her other hand began working the oil deep into my ass crack.

This wasn't like any muscle massage I'd ever heard about before.

"This okay?" she whispered. It was polite of her to ask.

My soft sigh turned into an embarrassing moan, which she took as an invitation to push deeper. She kept working on me like that until my cock was so hard that it was uncomfortable lying on it. She sensed it, and with one hand cupping my ass and the other under my waist, she tossed me onto my back. She might have been small, but there was nothing weak about her.

She moved so that her side was next to mine, flashed her tongue ring at me once, then pulled my cock into her mouth. Alternately, she'd use the tongue ring to tease the underside of my shaft, and her lips to kiss and peck. Suddenly she smothered my cock with her mouth, sucking it gently into her throat—all while her hands tugged at my balls and a lone finger darted and danced beneath them.

I never came so hard before. My orgasm rattled my insides and sent a rush of air into my head. She didn't expect so much out of me and lost the last gush. It dribbled onto her lips until she wiped it into her palm and the crevices formed by her fingers.

It took me a minute to recover. For that while, I couldn't even talk. But I sent a couple of silent thanks to my agent Ronnie for referring me to this place. By the time I said, "Wow," Nicki had cleaned up and put her shirt back on.

"How do you feel? Your back?" she asked.

"Great!" Actually, it felt so normal that I'd forgotten all about it. "What'd you do?"

"This wasn't a problem with your back. It was stress. You just needed to relax."

I sat up on the table and glanced at my watch. An hour ride home, even if I didn't get lost. I'd be missing a lot of the game. It was worth it.

"Got somewhere to go?" Some of the oil was seeping through her top.

"I did. No problem. Just wanted to catch the game."

"The big game?"

"Yeah," I admitted. Of course.

"I'm off work now. Going to a nearby sports bar to watch it. Just five minutes down the street. Want to join me?"

I couldn't believe she asked. But I didn't want to blow it by looking too eager.

"Several fifty-inch plasma TVs," she added.

I jumped on that. "Sure!"

"I'll just be a minute," she said. "If you want to go ahead and make sure we get a place to watch. It's bound to be crowded."

"Yeah. Sure. Just tell me where to go."

"It's easy to find. Just go up this street, make a right, and it's next to the day spa."

"Day spa?!"

"Yep. Best one on the West Coast. Lots of Hall of Famer guys go there."

E. Eliott

JennaTip #5: Happy Endings

In case you live under a rock, at the end of a massage if you are offered a "happy ending," that's the kind of massage in this story, the kind in movies, the kind a lot of people fantasize about.

Don't think that you'll get this kind of treatment at just any spa or massage place. You'll be sorely disappointed, not to mention embarrassed, if you go to a licensed massage therapist and roll over with a nice big stiffy poking up through the sheet because she or he just isn't going to do you any favors.

You have to do your research to find the right girl. You're more likely to get your "happy ending" if you look in the alternative papers and select someone offering erotic massage. Lots of times they come to your home for the massage, or if you're traveling, to your hotel.

If you go to a spa for one, you want to wait until the "happy ending" is offered or just ask over the phone before you even make an appointment to avoid unpleasantness. If you're in the wrong place and she's not that kind of girl (or he's not that kind of guy), you're likely to be tossed out on your ass for asking.

Now, for the girls, sometimes you can get a bit more out of the massage with some moans, groans, and subtle moving, getting a little finger play maybe, but it's unlikely you'll get the whole enchilada. The moaning and groaning may work with both guys and girls, but again, proceed with caution.

This story is totally different from anything else and very
sexy. The argument that love is about the person and not
the equipment is a powerful one for a lot of people.

Testing the Theory

The show was better than I'd expected—not brilliant but good enough, all things considered. As I was leaving, I bumped into my gorgeous young friends, Nigel and Rupert, so we just had to go for drinkies at The Grapes, which is just around the corner from the theater. Rupert got the drinks: a Cosmo for me, Cointreau on the rocks for Nigel, and a single malt for himself. The darling boy never forgets what anyone drinks and doesn't hesitate to provide same. That's not why I love him, but it certainly contributes.

The show's musical director was a mutual friend, so we allowed that his work was just short of adequate and concentrated our verbal venom on the sets, dancing, costumes, and performances.

I commented that the male lead's dancing just about qualified him to play Widow Twanky in *Aladdin*, provided it wasn't a West End production.

Nigel said, "You are such a bitch, Cynthia! I love it. If you were male, and gay, I'd do you in a shot."

"How would Rupert feel about that?"

"Me, too, darling. We both would."

I said, "I'm flattered, I think. Ditto, darlings. I'd do you, either or both, and you wouldn't have to change sex or sexual preference, either."

Rupert said, "But you're bi, Cynthia. We're gay, through and through. That makes a difference."

I gave Rupert my best smoldering look, then transferred it to

Nigel. "I fuck people whom I care for, regardless of their anatomy. So much of it is the same, what's the problem?"

Rupert leaned forward in his chair. "You don't have a cock, darling. That's quite a big difference."

Nigel commented, "It's a very big difference in your case, Rupert."

I said, "I have lips, a tongue, hands, and a bum. You two have the same. So, I have a pussy and you don't. You two have cocks and I don't. We're still more alike than not. Come to that, I imagine that to a cock, a pussy would feel like a cross between an anus and a mouth."

"Interesting," Nigel drawled. "I wouldn't know, never having tried one—pussy, that is."

I gave him an "up from under" look. "I thought you'd tried everything, Nigel."

The barman interrupted with, "Time, gentlemen and ladies, please."

Rupert frowned. "Shame. I do love to debate bedroom philosophy."

"We could go on somewhere," I suggested.

He shook his head. "Anywhere that's still open, you couldn't hold a conversation for the twittering of the twits."

Nigel laid an elegantly manicured finger on his lover's wrist. "We could take Cynthia home with us, Rupert, no? Then we could debate all night if we were so moved."

Rupert raised a subtly plucked eyebrow. "A sleepover? That might be fun, if you're up for it. Cynthia?"

Was I up for spending the night with two shockingly handsome, tall, muscular, gay young men? My feelings about it were much the same as a man's would be if a pair of lovely lipstick lesbians asked him to join them in bed. I hesitated, just for form's sake.

Nigel wheedled, "We have absinthe."

Rupert added, "From Germany."

"That's stronger, isn't it?" I asked.

"Three times the wormwood."

"Then how could I refuse?"

"We really didn't think you could," Rupert finished.

I drove. They rely on taxis. Their flat didn't disappoint me. The walls were pale pink. There were crimson carpets on the black parquet floor. The furniture was black leather, with an enormous sectional couch and several heavy club chairs. Even the oversize coffee table was padded and covered with black leather.

"Nice place for an orgy," I commented.

Nigel grinned. "It is intentional."

"I'll prepare the absinthe," Rupert announced. "How do you take yours, Cynthia?"

"Short, please."

He nodded his approval. Half spirits and half water with one cube of sugar is the connoisseur's preference.

"While you do that, is there someplace I could refresh myself? It's been a long day and I'm feeling grubby."

Nigel told me, "The guest bathroom is through there. If you'd like, take a shower, seeing as it's to be a sleepover. We don't have jammies to lend you but you'll find a robe hanging behind the door."

I really liked the way the evening was progressing. There was a shower cap that I helped myself to so I was able to wash and wrap my naked bod in a fluffy white robe and get back to my hosts in under fifteen minutes. They'd taken advantage of my brief absence to change into their own robes. Rupert's was a floor-length Victorian brocade in red and gold. Nigel wore a short pale blue silk wrap that showed his legs off nicely. My suspicions that they'd already decided to experiment with bisexuality were confirmed by the broad black leather collar with brass studs that was buckled around Nigel's throat. It was hardly the sort of thing a gentleman would wear for an evening of polite chitchat.

We toasted each other with virulent green absinthe. Nigel sat on the edge of the coffee table and tugged his wrap down just too late to stop me catching a glimpse of his dangling balls. That meant that either his cock was very tiny, or it was angled upwards in anticipation. Otherwise, I'd have seen it before his wrist trapped it.

"Now where were we in our philosophical discussion?" Rupert asked. "You were comparing pussies to mouths and bums, I believe, Cynthia."

"I was making the point that if people are attractive and affectionate, gender becomes a secondary issue at best."

"In an ideal world, I'm sure you'd be right."

"This is our ideal world, Rupert," Nigel said. "Here, in our little flat."

Rupert looked me up and down with a twinkle in his eye. "Despite what the Greeks claimed, some philosophical points can best be proved or disproved by experimentation." He stretched out to me to tuck in a vagrant curl. His fingertip, brushing the rim of my ear, made me shiver. "Is that what you had in mind, Cynthia?"

Suddenly, and uncharacteristically, shy, I nodded.

"Just so this isn't merely about prurient curiosity and is to be entered into in a true scientific spirit, why not?" He reached out to Nigel, took hold of his collar, and dragged him unceremoniously to his feet.

I held my breath. Strong, masculine lips parted. Without their mouths touching, each extended his tongue to lick and lap at the other man's. It was so hot. There's something about men kissing men that really turns me on. Seeing their tongues makes it even better. I looked down between them. Nigel's cock, very pale, quite thin but generously long, was jutting from his wrap like a flagpole. I braced myself. If I was going to join in the action, the sooner I made my presence felt, the better. If they got too wrapped up in each other before I joined in, I'd feel like an intruder.

I downed my absinthe and reached between the men. My right hand took hold of Nigel's shaft. My left parted Rupert's robe, reached in, and tugged out a darker, thicker, but equally long length of feverish flesh. I do like the feel of a hard hot cock in my hand. Having two to hold was more than twice as good because it was so much more depraved.

I stroked, slowly and gently. I was certain Rupert wouldn't be spooked by my touch. I wasn't so sure about Nigel. As I caressed those throbbing shafts, I made sure that their glistening heads rubbed together. The tie of my robe came loose. I let it flap open, not being obtrusively naked but leaving myself available, should anyone feel like pawing my goodies.

The boys' kisses became more intense. Nigel was panting. I was just beginning to worry that my fists' strokes might cause a premature climax to the proceedings when Rupert pushed down on Nigel's collar, forcing him to sit on the edge of the coffee table and plucking his cock from my fingers.

With one hand hooked into Nigel's collar and the other knotted in his hair, the dominant partner pulled the submissive one's face down to his cock. Nigel's lips parted. Rupert impaled Nigel's mouth and kept pulling, drawing the boy's lips down his shaft until his nose pressed against Rupert's stomach.

Both boys, I realized, were as clean shaven down there as I was.

Nigel was making little gurgling noises. I've made similar sounds myself, when a nice big cock has pushed its way to the back of my throat, as Rupert's had to Nigel's. I had to give the boy credit. Rupert was pushing and pulling on Nigel's head, face-fucking his young lover, and Nigel was taking it like a man, or perhaps like a woman.

They were making my point for me—that to a cock, a mouth is a mouth. A cock's owner might care about the sex of the mouth it's fucking but the cock itself doesn't.

I really enjoyed watching but participating would be even better. I dropped to my knees. There was some space between the boys, as Nigel was seated on the edge of the coffee table and Rupert was standing almost still, in effect, using Nigel's mouth to masturbate. The gap gave me room to get my head between them and take Nigel's cock between my lips. From what he'd said earlier, it had to be the first time a woman had ever fellated him. I'd been concerned that Nigel might have been skittish about having a woman wrap her lips around his cock. As it was, he couldn't have objected even if he'd wanted to, not with his mouth being pumped by Rupert's stiff flesh.

With Nigel leaning forward to serve Rupert, I didn't have a lot of room. All I could get into my mouth was the tasty head and half the stiff shaft of his fine young cock. That was fine by me. Mumbling on and tonguing a nice cock are different pleasures than having one shoved to the back of one's throat as it is done much more leisurely, less urgently. I like it both ways. In fact, when it comes to cocks, I like them any way I can get them.

My left hand stroked up the back of Rupert's muscular thigh. His bottom was tensing and relaxing. I found the pad of muscle at the base of his spine and let a finger trail down from there. The flexing of his hard flat buns trapped the tip of my finger. His muscles relaxed, which I took as an invitation. An inch lower, I felt the striated flesh of his sphincter. My finger stiffened and probed, rotating as it pushed. Nice! I very gently finger-fucked

Rupert's arse as he fucked Nigel's face and I suckled on the tip of Nigel's cock. Combinations like this are what make orgies so much fun, don't you think?

Rupert stiffened and pulled back, plopping his cock from between Nigel's lips. I was afraid for a moment that Rupert was about to climax but he's not that young. Nudging me aside, he took hold of Nigel behind his knees and lifted until Nigel was bum-up, ankles over Rupert's shoulders. His cock lay along his hard flat belly with its head resting on his navel.

Rupert told me, "Lube—top right drawer—sideboard."

I found it, in with a jumble of assorted toys, mainly butt plugs. The jar's label read RASPBERRY TINGLE. I took it to Rupert. He held his hand out. I said, "Allow me." Two of my fingers dipped in and scooped out a good dollop of the pink cream. I massaged it around and on Nigel's pucker. He clenched at first but gradually relaxed as the sensations got to him. Encouraged, I scooped out more and worked two fingers into the tight heat of his back passage.

Rupert said, "You've got a woman's fingers stuck up your arse, Nigel. How does it feel? Has Cynthia proved her point?"

Nigel pouted. "I want your cock, Rupert, please?"

I can take a hint. I scooped more lube, slathered it on Rupert's cock, and took a grip on his shaft. He nodded and bent at his knees a little. I forced his cock's head down and guided it. When its head was nestled in place, Rupert leaned, letting his weight slowly drive his cock into his lover's bum. Nigel grunted. Rupert pulled back an inch, then rammed down. Nigel grunted again. After half a dozen short hard strokes, Rupert pulled way back, far enough that only half the bulb of his cock was still inside Nigel, then pushed in again, taking his time, under perfect control.

You have to admire that in a man, don't you? Being self-controlled when he's fucking, I mean.

Not to be left out, I coated a finger of my left hand and my right palm with Raspberry Tingle, forced the finger all the way up Rupert's arse, and hand-stroked Nigel's cock. Rupert grinned at me. The way we three were tangled, his face and mine were only inches apart. I closed the gap, offering my lips. Darling Rupert accepted and pretty soon we were swapping spit like teenagers in the back seats of a cinema. It occurred to me that Rupert had been very quick to take my challenge. He and Nigel had been lovers for over four years and to the best of my knowledge, faithful to each other. Rupert, at least, had been ripe for a little nonthreatening experimentation.

His back passage clamped on my finger. Once more I suspected he was about to climax. Once more, I was wrong.

He pulled out of Nigel, leaving the poor boy writhing with lust, and lowered his legs so that his feet found the floor. Rupert leaned close to my ear and whispered, "Now's your chance."

Indeed it was. Nigel's cock was standing and stiff. Swiftly, I put my right knee on the table and threw my left leg over him. Rupert reached under me, took Nigel's cock in his hand and held it firmly for me to skewer down on. Nigel's eyes bulged with the shock of having his cock thrust into a pussy but as Rupert was fondling his balls he was forced to accept the invasion. Though I don't think invasion is the correct word, as it was my pussy that was invaded. His eyes closed. I didn't think he was up for a woman's kiss yet, so I arched over him to nibble on a nut-hard nipple and began to wriggle on his cock.

Rupert's hand on my bum stilled me. I felt his lube-coated fingers explore between my cheeks. My sphincter relaxed. One, two, three strong fingers pushed into me. They worked, massaging Nigel's shaft through the membrane that divides my rectum from my vagina.

"Feel that, Nigel?" Rupert asked.

Nigel's neck arched. He moaned.

"He can feel it," I said.

"It'll be good, darling," Rupert said. I assumed the endearment was meant for Nigel.

I held still for Rupert as he replaced his fingers with the plum of his cock and did that long slow thrust thing of his. It was close to devastating. Neither of them was exactly underendowed and having one cock in my pussy and another up my arse stretched me deliciously. Rupert gripped my hips and started pumping. Nigel lay still for a while but the sensations, being in my clenching pussy and feeling his lover's cock rub over his, eventually got to him. He began to hump up at me.

There's no way three people can coordinate their fucking. I just braced myself and held still, apart from contracting my internal muscles, alternating rectum and vagina. We began to sweat, all three of us. You know that the sex is good when everyone sweats. It's like eating a first-class curry.

Rupert's broad chest was sliding over my back. I was pressed down on Nigel, almost squelching. Neither of them had touched my titties but it was our first encounter. We'd get to that someday, I was sure.

Nigel's face screwed up. Rupert was grinding, hard, rotating his hips and straining to pierce me one last inch deeper. Both were very close. If they'd come inside me—rather—if Rupert had come in my bum, Nigel might have found it threatening. I heaved back at Rupert and slid sideways off Nigel. Their cocks were only inches apart. I took Nigel's in my right hand and Rupert's in my left. Pulling them head-to-head, I managed to work both into my mouth. A dozen or so quick hard pumps brought Rupert off and the gushing of his jism over the head of Nigel's cock, inside my mouth, tipped the boy over the edge.

I staggered back, gulping and licking my lips.

Rupert sank into a chair. "Cynthia," he said, "I think you've proven your point."

I shrugged. "It isn't scientific to rely on a single experiment."

"True," he said. "How about a little more absinthe first? Then we can repeat."

"But with variations," I agreed. "I've got a strap-on in my car."

"Interesting." Rupert turned to Nigel. "My dear boy, I don't think you've ever been buggered by a woman, have you?"

Diane Yves

Twenty Licks

It was almost as dark inside the motel room as out. Okay. We didn't need lights. We didn't even need to say much. Just tore off each other's clothes on our way to the bed. I took a few seconds to admire his tattoo. A multicolored dragon covered his entire back. I showed him mine: two stars right above both hipbones.

His body was as firm as I'd expected. But it felt even better. He was nice and clean. Clean-cut. Clean-shaved. Clean-smelling. Defined muscles. I could almost feel the tan lines where his shirt collar and sleeves had been. And I liked how his pale glow contrasted with my deep brown skin.

He picked me up and tossed me on the mattress, then tugged my black thong down to my knees. I kicked it the rest of the way off as his smile showed that he liked how firm my body was. All the exercise had given me that lean, hungry look. Slender torso, defined arms, tight waist.

He covered my entire body with wet kisses. I grabbed his hair, pushing his face between my legs but he spent just a few seconds there giving me what I term Lip Service. I tried to grind up against him, put that sweet little white boy mouth to good use, but he just lifted away, knee-walked up until he straddled my face, and pressed his thick cock against my lips. "Suck me," he demanded.

"Get off." I pushed him to the side and onto his back. I grabbed his cock and ran my tongue against his shaft, lower. He was so smooth. No pesky hairs to tickle my nose or get in my mouth. I took him deep, feeling his head hit the back of my throat. I milked his cock, tasting him, sucking him hard.

"Damn, girl. You're going to make me come."

I took him out of my mouth, stroked him with one hand. "Not on your life. Me first."

Before he could respond, I climbed on top of him. It'd been a while since I rode a thick one. It was a tight fit, but it felt just right after a thrust or two. Steadying my right hand on his chest, I bounced on his hard cock with my left hand between my legs, circling my hooded clit and jacking myself off.

By the time I was done with him, he was screaming louder than I was. We accidentally broke a lamp, knocking a dusty painting off the wall. And probably woke up the traveling salesman on the other side of the wall. I was worried that the lumpy old bed would collapse from all the bucking and thrusting. The bed made it. Barely.

And then, even before my heartbeat and breath had steadied, he closed his eyes, rolled over, and began to snore.

Shit. After two months, all I got was two beers and one fuck?

I wasn't too smart when I changed careers a few days before my twenty-first birthday. Sure the benefits were great. And it was a regular paycheck where I didn't have to pick berries or push an ice cream cart—like my parents had to do. Oh, and the on-the-job training. Better than any technical college could offer. And free.

So, I enlisted.

I wasn't ready for boot camp. Really didn't have much an idea of what it would be like. I guess I pictured it as summer school with guns.

But not for long.

The drill instructors didn't like anything about anything, but especially it seemed they didn't like anything about me.

They didn't like the length of my dark hair, and they had it cut so short, and so bad, that it looked like I had a pad of browned lettuce on my head. And they didn't like all my jewelry, so they took it away. They took my gum. They took the fashion magazines I brought. They took my matches and cigarettes. They even took my icy-blue-eyed contacts and gave me a pair of thick, geek glasses instead.

Things only got worse after that. Mostly because of Drill Sergeant Drexel.

He was harder to please than my mother. And he purposely mispronounced my last name: Diaz, as Dee-Ass. Just the slightest little thing would set him off. Then he'd stand there with his fists on his hips, screaming at me while his face turned red and his eyes tripled in size, his voice pitching high and low in all the wrong spots.

"Dee-Ass, why did you drop your M-16 A2 rifle in the mud?" he'd shout.

Or, "Dee-Ass why is your footlocker open?"

Or, "Dee-Ass, are you eyeballin' me?"

And after every one of his silly questions, he added, "Now drop and give me twenty."

Either he was the nastiest, hardest drill instructor ever, or I was the worst recruit.

I even tried to quit once. Dumb. Dumb. Dumb mistake.

I went up to Drill Sergeant Drexel, sobbing, and complained about my cracked nails, sores on my feet, and the food. Oh, God. The food was awful. Some fresh tomatoes, a little cilantro, and some onions might have made it tolerable.

This was the first time I saw him laugh. Then he was shouting again.

"Dee-Ass, you no-good, lazy, 'blah, blah, blah.' You don't

belong in the same uniform as, 'blah, blah, blah.' You are a little piece-of-shit, piece of pussy!"

Whoa! I had cousins who would kill any man they heard talk to me like that.

"Now drop and give me twenty!" Drill Sergeant Drexel yelled in my face.

But my cousins weren't there. Mom and Dad were a thousand miles away. My friends wouldn't recognize me in this haircut and without my makeup. All I had was me.

Me and the other recruits.

So, fine. If this asshole wanted me to do twenty more pushups, I would. And I dropped and I did them pushups crisp. Faster than I ever had before.

When I jumped back onto my feet, Drexel was gone.

Within two weeks I was running faster than any of the other women. I memorized all the rules and, well, they weren't all as silly as I first thought. I became as good at taking apart the M-16 A2 rifle and putting it back together again as I was with a nail file and curling iron. I still hated the food, though.

When I was ordered to do pushups, I did them. And I learned to like them. I liked how they flattened my tummy, broadened my shoulders, and made my ass tuck in. Eventually I started doing pushups even when I wasn't ordered to do them.

Basic was over before the sores on my feet had healed. And when I was packing up my stuff, Drill Sergeant Drexel marched up to me and said, "I never thought you'd make it . . . Blah, blah, blah." Then he stuck out his hand, and I shook it.

I could go anywhere I wanted on my time off after that, as long as I paid for travel. What I really wanted was a cold beer and a hard cock. So I hopped on a bus and headed to the nearest city.

When I entered the small bar, all eyes were on me. My short hair was a contrast to the few other women there; my build now as buff as most of the guy-straws sitting at the bar. Their skin was tanned red and mine was bred brown. Or, maybe it was the uniform?

I hopped on a bar stool and ordered a cold draft. Sipped my beer quietly while a crew of frat boys looked me over. Just like I figured, they were pussies. Too soft. They went elsewhere.

After twenty minutes, someone took the seat next to me. "Buy you a drink?"

If I had a dollar for every time some white boy asked me that, I wouldn't need the military pension. I looked him over but didn't respond. He was too All-American for my tastes. Natural blond, blue eyes, perfect teeth, but the thick forearms and a forty-inch chest made me look twice.

He opened his mouth to try something witty. I put up my hand. "Shut the hell up, and buy me a beer." That made him grin and flag down the bartender.

Blondie looked better after the next drink. He paid for the beer, and I paid for the room. Result: hot sex just before he rolled over and fell asleep.

So, after two months, all I got was two beers and one fuck? I slapped that cowboy on his bare ass. He shot up and stared at me with his lazy eyes.

"What the fuck do you think you're doing?" I huffed.

"Huh?" He shook the sleep off his face.

"Are you eyeballin' me?" I shouted, my voice rising and falling in all the wrong spots.

"No . . . what?"

"You pansy-ass, no good, lazy fuck. You think I'm here for my damn health?" I yelled. I was really enjoying this. It was getting me off.

"Get up and put your face between my legs right now, numb-nuts," I barked.

And he complied.

Then, with a low voice coming deep from my throat, I ordered, "Now drop and give me twenty."

Olivia Ulster-Reed

JennaTip #6: Clean Shaven Men

There is something very nice about a smooth face, a smooth chest, and smooth cock and balls.

Just like with a woman, it's neat and tidy. A lot of people think it looks nicer. It does cut down on odor and there aren't any little curlies left about on the soap. If you want to try it out (or want your guy to try it), keep in mind everything doesn't have to come off to make an improvement. For example, the chest area can just be trimmed down as opposed to shaved smooth. Shaving all the hair off can lead to stubble, itching as it regrows, and it takes a lot of upkeep.

Then there's the balls and cock. A beard trimmer works nicely on getting rid of any bushy areas, making it all nice and short. Leave it that way or take it all off. This area isn't quite so large (no offense) as the chest, so it's easier to keep it smooth if that's the look and feel you are going after. First buzz cut the area, then go for the razor finish for a smooth, soft scrotum. The triple-blade razors, like the Mach 3, work really well.

Some guys may elect to wax, but if you shave well, and keep it up (no one wants razor rash from stubble there), it doesn't have to come to that.

I had mixed responses to this story but thought it worth including. Hope you are one of the ones that likes it like I did.

Snow Job

"Shit, it's cold." I shivered. It wasn't a lie.

"Pussy. Shut up. We'll be fine." Derrick was trembling as much as I was.

Neither of us had been through a New England winter before—never mind a blizzard. He wasn't used to driving through all this white crap. And when we hit that patch of ice, he swung the steering wheel in all the wrong directions, sending us into a small glacier.

We spent nearly two hours trying to rock and roll the car out of the frozen wave of snow. I pushed. He pushed. And the whole while, the gas pedal was pressed to the floor. All we did was burn rubber and waste gas. Eventually, of course, we ran out of fuel. We were totally stuck by then.

The heater blew cold air as the frigid wind pushed in through the windows. The snow and ice under the car radiated cold like a reverse oven.

"Fuck, even my nuts are ice," said Derrick.

"No one else is dumb enough to be out on this road tonight. We'll die. Right here. If we don't do something."

"We can make a fire. You got matches or a lighter?" Derrick knew that neither of us smoked and he'd tossed the car lighter out and used the hole for running his phone charger.

"Maybe we should hike for it. How far can it be to a house or something?"

"We took a wrong turn off the highway. Could be hours of walking. We'd never make it in this." Derrick was usually a macho son of a bitch. Now, he sounded like a quitter.

"I'm cold." I wrapped my arms around myself.

"Me, too."

"Maybe we should get close. Conserve our body heat." I thought it was a good idea. Neither of us had dressed in any more than jeans and T-shirts.

"Are you fucking gay?" Derrick slid his ass right against the driver's door and stuck his sneaker between us.

"Wait," I hushed.

"Just stay the fuck on your side of the car."

"What's that?" I saw snow glowing in the distance. Maybe a low-flying UFO? Or the moon reflecting off ice? No! It was headlights! A pickup truck appeared, kicking out snow, dirt, and ice in its wake as it skidded and swerved from one side of the white-carpeted road to the other. The truck whizzed straight by us, then came to a stop about thirty feet away.

"All right!" I applauded as Derrick coughed out a frosty laugh.

The driver got out and walked toward us. He was a big guy, covered top to bottom in winter clothes—a bulky, green parka with a hood that funneled around his face, thick mittens, pants packed so tight with thermals that the wrinkles were solid, and knee-high storm boots.

I followed Derrick out of the car as the snowman neared. The cold wind stung so hard that we hopped from one foot to the other as our palms held our elbows.

The truck driver examined our car.

"We got stuck. In the snow," I offered. Like it wasn't obvious.

"Ran out of gas trying to get out," Derrick added.

The truck driver didn't need to know any more than that before he was stomping back to his truck and waving for us to follow. On the way, Derrick slipped and fell on his ass and elbows. When I tried to help him up, he pushed me away.

Soon, we were inside the truck's cab, me in the center. Our savior, thankfully, blasted the heat for us before driving off. For a short while, the way the truck was all over the road, I thought the driver was having trouble. But then I realized that he really was just having fun. He knew exactly how to handle the snow and ice. He knew how his tires and truck would react to the conditions. He wasn't as much driving as he was dancing.

Just as I was about defrosted, the truck tore into a partially plowed driveway that led to a small log cabin. The driver parked under a patch of white-blanketed evergreens and stopped.

I took the opportunity to say, "Thanks." A word that Derrick repeated, but more quietly.

That's when the driver pulled off the parka's hood and smiled.

"No problem," she said. "It's fun to go out and rescue people."

It wasn't just that she was a woman. No. She was hot. The right combination of cute and sexy. Sparkling blue eyes, pert nose, wide smile. She was pale like she didn't get much sun. She slipped her hood down and shook out her long blond hair. I'd say she was a natural blonde. Just my type.

"Come on in." She opened her door. "I'll get a fire started and lend you some blankets. Do you guys like beer?"

Derrick and I raced each other to the cabin's front door. Inside, our hostess lit the entire fireplace up, gave us warm blankets and a six-pack of green-bottled beer. While Derrick and I sat on the couch, absorbing the fire's glow, she went off to dress herself down.

Derrick cleared his throat when she came back. I looked up and almost choked on my brew. She glided toward us, long legs peeking through the slits of her white robe. It was made of a soft material, maybe silk or satin. She had barely tied it closed, giving us a good look at her full cleavage, her hard nipples poking through the fabric.

She sat on the couch between us, stretching her legs in front of her. I handed her a fresh beer. She smiled, touched my arm to say thanks. Leaned close to give me a better look at her breasts.

I looked away. "Thanks again for saving our asses."

Derrick's laugh sounded nervous. "Yeah. We'd have been popsicles by now."

She laughed and touched Derrick's face. "Too cute," she said. With her other hand, she squeezed my thigh. When she kissed Derrick, I didn't know what to do. It was obvious that she'd made her choice. Derrick got the girl, and I'd have to settle for the rest of the beer. Should I sneak off? Give them some privacy? When I shifted my weight away from them, she gripped my thigh harder.

Her blue eyes looked right into me. "Where do you think you're going?"

"I . . . uh . . ." My voice shook a little. I never saw myself as a threesome type of guy. From Derrick's glare, I knew he wasn't either. I thought maybe we should flip a coin.

Our hostess stood to face both of us. She smiled and opened the tie of her robe and let it fall. A peek below confirmed that I was right. She was a natural blonde.

Her lips curled into a smirk as she sat back down between us. "If you're going to thank me, you might as well do it right."

Derrick and I looked at each other, then we looked away. I'm sure we were thinking the same thing—that the couch suddenly felt awfully crowded.

I had no idea what I was doing or how to start up a three-some. But I didn't have to. She took charge like this wasn't her first time. She leaned over Derrick and unzipped him. His cock sprung out, almost hitting her lips. She smiled and stroked it with one hand, licking the tip. It seemed so natural that I didn't realize I was staring until Derrick growled at me.

Too late though. My cock was already responding to the live blow job, growing hard and pressing against my inside fly.

She shifted onto the sofa. Her mouth was still on him, but now she was on all fours with her ass pointing at me. I caressed her thighs, her ass, moving my fingers between her legs. God, she was slick. Two, then three fingers easily went into her. She responded by taking Derrick's cock deeper into her mouth. She gagged every time his cock hit the back of her throat.

The two of them worked in tandem as she removed Derrick's belt buckle and pulled his pants past his thighs. I stood and took off my own, figuring that I'd soon look damn out of place if I didn't. Derrick repositioned his ass on the couch's arm while I knelt behind her. Her mouth dove back onto Derrick's cock as my fingertips searched for her wet spot. She moaned when I found her clit again. Then she wiggled her ass and thighs, sucking my fingers into her.

Derrick started making hard-to-ignore noises. Loud huffs scratched his throat and curled his tongue. She became even more spirited as my fingers worked on her, her thighs trembling and her ass making wide circles. I was more than invited, I was commanded.

My cock slid easily inside her and, for a moment, she stopped sucking on Derrick to let out a throaty moan. She ground her ass against me as she took Derrick's cock again. Derrick's eyes flashed wide, staring straight into mine. Then he shut them back up, and I focused on the small of her back. I'd rather concentrate on her than look at him.

It was difficult fucking on the couch. The cushions were soft and exaggerated the pressure that my knees put on them. A couple times, I almost fell out of her and to the floor. To steady myself, I grabbed onto the side of her ass with one hand. Held her tight while I fucked her.

One of her hands reached back and grabbed mine. With our fingers interlocked, it was almost intimate. For a second, I forgot about Derrick. I was able to thrust harder and rhythmically, timing my strokes with the trio of heightening breaths and shivering limbs.

I came. Two pumps inside her, the rest dribbling down the inside of her thighs as my hand tightened hard onto hers. Derrick came about the same time. I could hear her swallowing his come with loud gulps.

My erection had barely begun to droop when Derrick's cold voice snarled, "Let go of my fucking hand."

"Sorry." I lost my grip and pulled myself over to the opposite end of the couch.

Derrick and I finished up the beer. Then we must have passed out, each on our own end of the couch.

The next morning, we both woke, groggy. We couldn't find the girl anywhere, but with the weather a little better and the sun peering through the clouds, we could see that the little cabin was not too far from a local motel. We found some flannel shirts and sweatshirts in the cabin and borrowed them to make the walk. Her truck was nowhere around.

When we got to the motel, we checked in—separate rooms—and slept the rest of the day and night away. By the next afternoon, the storm had cleared entirely and we felt ready to rescue the car and try getting on our way. Most of the main roads were plowed down to black asphalt, so we hired a tow-truck driver to drive us back to our car, fill up the tank, and pull us out of the snow.

While driving there we passed the small log cabin.

"Hey, I know that place!" I pointed.

"That place?" The driver didn't seem to believe me. "Been empty for years. No one ever goes near it."

"Why not?" I knew I'd regret asking.

"Haunted. Woman named Lenore used to live there. Very pretty. I remembered her back when I was in school. Her hobby was driving around in her pickup truck during snowstorms and rescuing the dumb bastards who got their cars stuck. Right up until one day she hit a deer and rolled off the road and through pond ice. Word is, her spirit comes back every snowstorm and drives around looking for people to save."

The rest of the ride was damn silent. After Derrick and I were back on the road, it was an hour later that I had to say something. The words had been banging around too long inside my mouth.

"Derrick, does that mean she wasn't really there?"

Derrick slammed on the brakes, swerved to the side, and stopped. Then he pointed a finger in my face and warned, "Don't ever say another fucking word about it."

Shoshanna Hedras

Playing dress-up any time of year (or day) can make for a lot of fun.

The Most Wonderful Time of the Year

When people ask me what my favorite holiday is, I always answer honestly, "Halloween."

"That's not a holiday," is the usual response.

"It is for me," I always say, smiling but adding nothing.

I'm slim, attractive, brainy. There's nothing extraordinary about me, really, except my multiorgasmic ability, which is so incredible one of my exhausted boyfriends once called me "megaorgasmic." I laughed, but I knew it was true.

One man can never bring me to that dreamy state of postorgasmic bliss, because he always conks out while I'm left with that nagging sense that I've still got one more climax left in me. But, I'm a serial monogamist. For 364 days of the year, that is. Halloween night is different. It's my night to go wild, to unleash the anonymous adventuress who seeks absolute fulfillment the only way I can get it, from a series of lovers.

I start planning very early—okay, almost as soon as Halloween ends. There's a lot to consider, and besides, it's fun. My costume must hide my identity, of course, and must be sexy. No pumpkiny, ghoulish, or clownlike costumes for me! I need an outfit that will attract all the men, so I can "work the crowd" all night long.

This year, I decided to be Salome, she of the dance of the

seven veils. I spend what I must to make my costume spectacular. My seamstress is a genius with a needle and thread and not averse to being paid in cash. So, when the hallowed night arrived at last, every piece of my outfit was perfect. Silk harem pants cuffed with hand-sewn sequins, in an exquisite shade of lavender. With, need I mention, elastic in the waistband? Bare midriff, of course, with a real amethyst tucked into my pierced navel. A slip of a silk bra, exquisitely decorated with seed pearls and more sequins. A yashmak to cover the lower half of my face, and seven gorgeous veils, all silk, in various shades of purple. Tiny, perfect silk slippers. Oh my God, it was such a beautiful outfit I mourned the fact that it would only be worn once, but that is always the case with my costumes.

I admit my earrings, the chains that looped my waist and the cuffs at my wrists, all "gold," were fake, but everything else, even the new belly jewel, was real.

My costume must be comfortable, as I discovered one year after a hoop skirt caused more trouble than it was worth, so rather than wear a black wig over my chestnut hair, I dyed it. Since I'd told my boyfriend I would be away at a conference for a week, there'd be time enough to dye it back before I'd see him again. My eyes are dark brown, and once they were lavishly painted with black eyeliner, dark, glittery eye shadow and six coats of mascara, they were as alluring as those of any real odalisque.

The venue is of utmost importance. Luckily I have a friend from our school days who is now a renowned artist and a recluse. She receives invitations every year to all the gala events, and gives me my pick of the parties. I've been to most of the best over the years, and this year was no exception. There's a castle in the city where I live, built long ago by some lovelorn millionaire, and a multinational corporation had rented it for the night. There'd be hundreds of guests, a plethora of men for me to choose from. Most likely there would not be one person I would know or who would know me. My pulse quickened at the thought of all the exotically garbed men who'd be jostling each other for a shot at Salome. My nipples hardened, and I'd made sure the silk bra had no beading in the center of the cups, so my arousal would be evident to all. Do I need to mention the state my clit was in? It practically begged for a quickie with my vibrator, but I dismissed the thought. Long sessions with a mechanical toy might be fine for other nights, but not this one.

I arrived at ten-thirty. Late enough to ensure a crowd but not so late that the party ended before I'd accomplished my goal. This one would go into the wee hours but then, so would I.

The party was in full swing but my entrance did not go unnoticed. I was almost feverish with need so I wasted no time. The main floor was decorated in a fifties theme. A tall sailor requested a dance during which I gyrated against him until he was stiff as a mast. When the dance ended, he "lured" me into the library and pressed me up against a wall of books. I let him suck my nipples for a few minutes but it was my clit that was screaming for attention. Once I freed his erection from his pants, he abandoned all pretense of seduction, shoved my harem pants down to my knees, and jammed his prick into my wet pussy. It was fast, frenzied, artless, and I loved every second of it. My clit rode that rod ecstatically.

It hardly mattered that he came in a matter of minutes, because my first orgasm was almost instantaneous. Every thrust detonated my lust. I shuddered, then gasped, then gripped his shoulders and came with a white-light intensity that almost left me limp . . . except for the ache for more that always immediately follows my climax. I think he was surprised but maybe not—his eyes were shut tight. He quickened his speed, took one hand off my bared breast, and braced himself against the books behind my head. Maybe he thought I might try to escape, now that I'd come, but he didn't know me. Where many women might experience a gradual calming sensation, my next orgasm grabs onto the tail of the previous one, so by the time he was grunting and grinding his way to fulfillment, I was riding high again. My second was as intense as my first, and so it would be for most of the night. If I was lucky, and I always am on Halloween, by the end of the night my climaxes would take longer to reach and shatter my senses when I got there, and then, maybe, start to lessen until finally, for a little while, I'm free of need.

His weight pressed against me. I slipped away, leaving him limp against the books. Now for my escape. I learned long ago not to linger. My biggest problem at these parties was avoiding the fellows I'd already fucked.

I ascended the grand staircase to the second floor. This time I'd be a little pickier. I fancied a vampire, they were always fun, and possibly a king. A superhero would fit the bill nicely. I'd go where the search for satiation and adventure led me.

The main room of the second floor was done up as a disco. Excitement fueled my body with adrenaline. The pounding music matched the thud of my heartbeat and I imagined I could feel my clit throbbing with my pulse to the same frenetic disco inferno. Even the glittering disco ball matched my mood. Colors danced across the gyrating bodies of monsters and movie stars, demons and heroes, the famous and the infamous. I'd yet to have a drink but I thirsted more for climax than champagne. I made as dazzling an entrance onto the dance floor as I dared, trailing a violet-hued scarf behind me. The music and the crowd enveloped me. I let the scarf go and started dancing with myself. Whoever brought me my scarf, I decided, would qualify as my hero of the night.

He was not a hero but an African king. My scarf was knotted

at his waist, already a part of his brief, batik loincloth. Bare, six-pack abs, decorated with war paint. A face chiseled from granite, also painted. Lips I could already feel mashed against my nether lips. He was more than six feet of marvelous, muscled man. Barefoot, if you can imagine.

We dirty danced. His cock was thick and hard under—barely under—his loincloth. I rode his muscled thigh to my third orgasm of the evening. It rose up in me like lava traveling the core of a volcano. I parted my lips so I wouldn't explode, but I kept my moaning low. Of course, he heard it. A smirk slid across his face, and I saw a trace of the lawyer or doctor who lived inside this warrior's body on every single night but this one. Not unlike how my need for many male partners to satisfy my lust was almost always kept safely under wraps. My third orgasm was barely over when I started craving my fourth.

I managed to grab a glass of champagne while he collected what appeared to be a real spear. I gulped the wine in two long, bubbly swallows that tingled all the way down to my belly, sending my clit the all-systems-go signal that it clamored for.

We stumbled into one of the bedrooms. He kicked the door shut behind him and fell on top of me on the bed. He tore off my yashmak with his teeth and took my mouth. The kiss was so sensual we both groaned and abandoned all pretense of foreplay. In seconds his thick, purple cockhead was nudging my nether lips aside. He took me in one long slow stroke that had my clit dancing with joy. His heavy balls spanked my ass, even more so once he pulled my knees up to his shoulders and plundered me mercilessly.

I found the sweet spot, the moment where my orgasms, one descending as the next ascends, meet. It is a millisecond of pure bliss. And because of my multi-ability, I experienced wave after wave of these perfect little moments.

He was a fabulous fuck, varying his rhythms and our positions as it suited him. He moaned plenty, as did I. Through a haze of happiness I heard his breathing turn to panting and knew he was heading for his well-deserved come. I wrapped my legs around his waist, locked my feet behind his back, and clung to his neck with both arms. I pressed my damp cheek to his and urged him on with husky groans. "I can take it, baby. Oh yeah, yeah, give it to me! You deserve it, you're the best. . . ." His orgasm was so intense it scared me, but I held on tight as he rode me to its end.

I admit, I actually checked his pulse before I left.

The third floor was rock and roll. I fell into the arms of the first handsome superhero I spied. It was Zorro who caught me, more hero than super, perhaps, but in my disheveled state I wasn't going to quibble. He carried me to one of the massive balconies, where he cuddled me in his lap and cooed compliments while reviving me with snacks and champagne. We had a lazy little lap-fuck while gazing at the stars. It was just the thing to perk me up enough to get to the fourth, and last, floor.

It was done up as Dracula's lair so I had my pick of handsome vampires. I chose the one whose costume was the most authentic. If there was a man among them whose taste for the juices of a woman went unmet every night but this one, I wanted to find him. This one was as courteous as a true count, and he promised to eat me all up.

Once we were in his private chamber he fell upon me. I succumbed, swooning into an ornate Louis Quinze chair. He knelt at my feet, removed my pants, and commenced feasting on my juicy cunt with the ravenousness of a man starved for it. He lapped and sucked at me until I was so consumed that my head lolled to one side and the flames in the massive stone fireplace were the only things I could see. He ate me until the only sign of orgasm was when my breathing rose to panting one more time, the ebbing response to the final tremors of my last orgasm. It rippled lightly through my body, like fingers delicately plucking the final notes of a piece of music from a harp, and I was done. Sucked dry by Count Dracula.

When I got home, I laughed out loud when I saw what condition I was in. My clit was swollen as big as a prune and much the same color. It matched the lavender hues of my costume beautifully, as did the bruises I'd managed to collect over the course of the night. I slept a solid twenty-four hours, the sleep of a woman fully sated. When finally I awoke, it was to begin planning my costume for the next year. What would I be . . . a masseuse, perhaps?

Isadore Thomas

JennaTip #7: When One Is Not Enough

Do you have an itch and your guy just can't seem to scratch it for you? Are you interested in recruiting a few back-up players for the game? Have a talk with your guy and let him know you are having cravings. You never know—he might be feeling the same way.

If he isn't, then you may be facing a decision. If you really like him, at least see if you can make it work by trying lots of new things with him. A little variety might be all you need.

You can also try playing pretend. Wear costumes, buy some wigs and disguises, set up situations to act out, like picking him up in a bar and fucking him in the parking lot.

You can also try some major flirting with someone else, maybe with a little foreplay that you and your guy agree to ahead of time, but you save the real deal for him.

There are a lot of ways to try to make it work without it having to *be* work.

If he's not too freaked with your suggestion of bringing in a relief pitcher, so to speak, still start slow. Either agree that it'll be anonymous and he won't have to know about it or talk about adding someone together. As with everything, talk together, make sure you both understand what it is you want and how you both feel, then go for it.

*The woman in this story is really strong! In fact, all the
stories are about powerful women who get what they want
in the bedroom (or the bus—but that's another story). It
takes a confident woman to submit, if that's what she has
to have sexually. Knowing what turns you on and what
you want from your partner is powerful.*

Personal Trainer

"Are you comfortable, Amanda?"

She wriggled, heaving her belly up and straining at the bonds
that stretched her ankles so far apart. "My tendons, Simon.
They ache."

"Then a slight change in position, perhaps?"

"Yes, please?"

"Of course." I took a pillow from the top of the bed, slid a
palm under her rump, lifted and pushed the pillow under her.

"That's worse," Amanda moaned.

"Yes, but different. If you could see how nice those taut
sinews up the insides of your thighs look, you'd be glad to be
stretched more."

"Would I?"

"If for no other reason than it pleases me. You do want to
please me, don't you?"

"Yes, but . . ."

I took a grip on the softness in the hollow of her left thigh
and pinched, my thumbnail biting deeply. Amanda writhed and
sobbed.

"No 'buts,'" I told her. "Do you want to please me?"

"Yes. Of course, Simon. I do."

"No matter what?"

She turned her head to wipe her tears on the sheet. "No matter what, Simon."

"I've bruised you," I remarked. "You have a nice little crescent bruise in your groin. Are you proud of your bruise?"

"Um, yes."

"Good bitch. You're learning. I'm going to give you more bruises, Amanda. What do you say to that?"

"Er—thank you?"

"Good. Now ask me to mark your sex, Amanda. Tell me that you want pain."

"If it pleases you, Simon, please mark me and give me pain."

"You learn quickly. For that, a small reward."

"Reward?"

"Pain soon, Amanda. For now, this." I knelt between her thighs. My loving fingertips stroked their glossy skin. I leaned closer, tongue extended, and laved the bruise with delicate wet licks. My cheek felt the warmth from the outer lips of her sex.

Amanda closed her eyes and bathed in the delicate sensations, my tongue, my saliva. The damaged skin was so much more sensitive now. The pain had made it tender and so incredibly responsive.

"Simon?"

"Yes?"

"That feels so good. Is it all right for me to tell you that?"

"Of course. You like your pubes to be licked?"

"Yes, Simon. Very much."

"Then . . ." I stood and showed her a sort of whisk. It was a short handle with a dozen dangling thongs, each very thin and each with a knot near the end. "After this, your mound is going to be incredibly sensitive, Amanda."

She strained to sit up. "Please, Simon, no! I want to please you, I really do, but please don't use that on me, not there!"

I said, "One day, if you are what I think you are, you will beg for the thong's lick, not just on your pubes but everywhere. The thong will bring your skin alive in ways you've never dreamed of, but for now . . ."

I slashed down. She grunted from the shock and the fear, but I knew it wasn't unbearable, as she'd likely thought it would be. It was like a splash of fire, intense for a fraction of a second, then warming and exciting.

"You mark nicely," I remarked just before the instrument descended again, and again, and again.

"Six," I announced at last.

She was sobbing uncontrollably but her pussy was weeping as well. Its glow had her on the brink of climax.

"Simon, thank you. Thank you for showing me. Please, just one more," she begged.

"Greedy little bitch! More later, if I decide to give you that, but not there, though."

"Am I allowed to ask where, Simon?"

I didn't answer. My tongue was wet and flat, slavering on the burn, cooling and soothing but inciting it to need.

"Where?" I asked at last. "Where else shall I beat you?" My fingertip pressed on the head of her clit, protecting it, and the whisk beat down again, setting the skin of her outer lips on erotic fire.

"Oh, Simon. Please don't!" she gasped.

"Don't?" I let my displeasure show in my voice at being contradicted.

"Please, Simon. Just don't damage me."

"I never damage."

The little stinging flail fell, again and again. This time it was enough to take her to one climax, then two. I was awed at the flood that poured out from between her lips.

I tossed the whisk aside and cupped my hand beneath her flooding cunt. Amanda compressed inside, spilling more of her tangy sweet juice. I came around to her head and bent low so she could see the pool in my palm before I slurped it between my lips.

I was drinking her. My mouth moved closer, over hers. Amanda parted her lips. A stream of her cum jetted from my mouth into hers before my lips descended and sealed on hers, to suck the sweet-salt spice back. Two, three, four times I exchanged the nectar with her until it was all gone.

"Did you know before right now, this very moment, how perverted you are?" I asked, grinning.

"No, Simon, I didn't. Thank you for showing me."

"And do you enjoy being educated in yourself, learning these things about who you really are?"

"Yes, Simon. But—"

"But? Is there really a 'but'?"

"No, Simon."

"Good bitch. I'm going to mark you again now." I strolled back to her spread thighs.

She tensed. "Simon, may I ask? Where?"

"Inside."

"Inside?"

"Like this." I lubricated the first two fingers of my right hand.

Amanda knew enough to relax her sphincter. Both of my fingers slid in up to their second joints. It distended her rectum but I'd put my cock in farther than that, and my cock is much wider than my two fingers. She'd find fingers pleasant, not even threatening. My left hand parted the lips of her sex. My pressure increased until the floor of her sex was forced up and forward, as if I were turning her sex inside out. She had to be on the edge of pain when I put my mouth to her wet flesh. I was kissing her, deeper inside than human lips had ever reached. I sucked hard.

"Simon! What are you doing?" She was practically screaming.

I pulled back. "I am marking you. And you won't have to wear a scarf to hide this mark. In fact, you'll need a mirror to even see it. It's a pretty one, I promise you."

"Simon. Thank you for the mark." She hestitated, then went on despite my scowling look, "Simon, I would like very much to feel you inside me. Would you please, please enter me?"

"You've asked very prettily, but I do not like being asked. I will enter you as I like. And right now, I like your ass."

She had the nerve to pout. "But we've done it before."

"How dare you, bitch." I slapped her red, swollen mound with the flat of my hand. She jerked but had the good sense to remain stoically silent.

"You want something new?" I demanded. "Today has not been interesting enough?"

"Simon, no. Of course that isn't what I meant at all. Today has been perfect because you are perfect. Whatever you wish will be exactly what I want and need. Thank you for teaching me." She went on a bit breathlessly. Although it was a long speech, it did only a little to mollify me.

"Simon, I just wish to learn everything and I am sorry for being impatient."

I decided to forgive her.

"Since you seek something new, let me introduce you to ben-wa."

"But Simon, I've used ben-wa—" A severe warning glance cut her off midsentence.

"I know, dear, but not the way I intend to introduce them." I couldn't help but smile as I pulled the ben-wa balls from the table behind me and showed them to her. The fear in her eyes nearly caused me to lose my iron will and control.

"You've never had ben-wa like these."

I rolled the two spheres on my palm. Staring at them, Amanda twitched, fascinated and horrified. Regular ben-wa are the size of marbles. These were—well, not as big as pool balls, but close. They chimed as they rolled because of the steel balls inside.

"But Simon, surely they will not fit," she protested.

"Ah, but they will. Leave it to me," I promised. "Anyway, that's the least of your problems."

She watched as I poured oil over the balls before taking them down to the aching gape of her stretched-open hole.

"Simon!"

I ignored her. Cold metal pressed against the soft cup of flesh. It rotated, pressing. She parted, opening. Her lips stretched. More pressure. She held her breath. The first ball was halfway in, almost painful but terribly exciting. More force—more—a twist— and her labia closed on it.

"Oh," she sobbed. "I didn't think it was possible."

"That's one," I said.

"Simon, no! There cannot possibly be room. I can't . . ."

There was a chink as metal touched metal, followed by a deep chime. I increased the pressure. The first ball worked higher, into the tight place where her vagina's mouth opened. Her pubic bone was in the way.

"There," I announced. "Just an adjustment now. I want the second ball to press against your g-spot."

My fingers worked into her, seemingly impossible because there was just no room. She was stretched, filled. My fingers manipulated, moving the second ball around.

I said, "Good! Try bucking."

Amanda obeyed. The balls collided and rang, sending soundless vibrations that she had to feel in her bones, her sex, her very womb. She cried, "Oh fuck! Oh Simon!" Amanda convulsed. Her abdomen writhed. Her vagina pumped orgasms, one after the other, flooding past the round intruders to squelch out and spill onto the edge of the bed.

Amanda squealed and cried. It was physically too much. She couldn't stop and she couldn't take any more.

"Simon. You've taken me over. I've lost all control of my own body." She wept uncontrollably.

"Exactly. Your body is mine. Now, as I said, I'm going to use your anus."

Amanda stopped weeping and stared at me, wide-eyed, as she asked, "Simon, you will remove the ben-wa first, won't you? Oh! No, Simon, no! Don't do that! Don't push your cock into . . . Oh! You're past the ring, Simon. You're in. Please, please! No more. Oh, nooooooooo! Oh, the ball is being pushed up against my G-spot again. I cannot take any more, Simonnn . . ." The last bit of my name was a wail as she came like never before.

Her head reared up on her craning neck. Her eyes blazed. "Enough, I tell you. It just isn't possssss. . . . Ah, ah, ah! Oh . . . Oh no! Not past the second ball, no, no, no please! Simon, you're a wonderful man and I'll do anything for you but plea*aaaaaase*! God, fuck, God, fuck, godfuck, godfuck . . . Oh nooooo. I'm coming and coming and I want to stop. Please make it stop, Simon! Please, by all that's holy, make it stop!"

When I'd withdrawn and worked the balls from her and released her bonds, I rocked her as she sobbed in my arms.

"You have so much to learn, Amanda."

"I know that, Simon. And you have to go back north and leave me."

"Take a weekend off next month."

"Yes, Simon. What do you want me to do?"

"Come north for a visit. The next step in your education will be by example."

"By example, Simon?"

"With my slutling. You are going to watch. You'll enjoy that. I am going to show you how much a real pain-slut can endure."

"And, Simon, she will not mind?"

"If it's relevant, no, she'll enjoy it. The fifteenth, then. I'll arrange your flight. Now sleep, Amanda. You must be . . . Oh. Too late." I turned her to lay on the bed at full length and tucked her in tenderly.

Tracy Randolph

JennaTip #8: Ben-Wa

There are a lot of myths about ben-wa balls. The truth is that they are for your PC muscle, the one that holds your uterus in and controls your orgasms. You also use it to stop yourself from peeing.

By strengthening these muscles, you increase the power of your orgasms. A lot of women do Kegel exercises, particularly after giving birth, to get control back. The ben-wa exercise the same area. The difference is that they are in there rolling around rather than you just clenching and relaxing your vagina while it's empty.

You have to clench to keep the balls from falling out. They aren't pool-ball size like in the story at all. They're not much bigger than a large gumball.

The ben-wa have weights in them and are heavy. If you don't work your muscle, they will just slide right out of you. Potentially, if you get in just the right position, you will be able to rock them into your g-spot, but there are some really great vibrators and dildos out there (and fingers) that are more direct about stimulating the g-spot. Try ben-wa if you want, but they are primarily for exercising your muscle. It is worth it, however, to get your PC muscle in good shape for some amazing, mind-blowing orgasms. A strong muscle leads to strong orgasms.

Guys can also learn a lot of control by working their muscle. Recommend that your guy stop and start his piss flow when he takes a leak. Guys who learn to have multiorgasms do it to train themselves. Yes. Guys can have multiorgasms. They have the feeling of an orgasm without the ejaculation. Now for a bit of trivia: In China they believed that each time a man ejaculated his life expectancy would drop, so they actively trained their bodies to orgasm without ejaculation.

Light . . . camera . . . action . . . and the perfect
Hollywood ending!

Writer's Cramp

I'd sold everything I owned. My duffel was packed with my toiletries, six pairs of boxers, my newest pair of black jeans, and ten identical black T-shirts. I put my eight best scripts into my briefcase, charged extra battery packs for my laptop, and caught an LA-bound bus out of Toronto. My plan was to work as I rode, but the bus was packed. It must have been a parents-with-screaming-kids special. I was squished between two squabbling families in the backseat and couldn't move, couldn't work, couldn't even think. Even scratching my nose required advance planning.

I changed buses in Detroit. In my rush to grab a vacant place in the back, I must have passed the girl without seeing her. The first time I noticed her it was just her leg, very long, very shapely, and projecting out into the aisle about four seats in front of me. I wondered how short her skirt was because she was showing me over half her thigh and there was no sign of fabric. Between creating brilliant scenes on my laptop, I checked the leg. Its foot was neatly shod in ballerina-style flats—sensible for traveling but still sexy. I decided to put something similar on the heroine of my script.

Chicago was a layover. I hurried to get off, hoping to catch her or at least a full-length look, but the aisle was blocked by an obese, sweating guy. When I passed her seat, it was empty. I grabbed a burger and a coffee with my eyes peeled. She was nowhere in sight.

Back in the bus, a soldier had taken her seat. Disappointed, I returned to mine, with my choice of backseats now that the bus was half empty. At the very last moment, she scurried aboard and swung down the aisle toward me. The leg hadn't lied. The rest of her matched. Her tightly belted flared skirt was tiny. She had kittenish hips and a narrow waist but her breasts, bouncing and swaying generously inside her clinging black sweater, really belonged to a woman twice her size. Honestly, my absolute type.

She had a cute face with swollen, beestung, kissable, nibble-able lips, and a head of bubbly blond curls.

She stopped right in front of me. I swallowed.

"Do you mind if I take the window seat?" she asked.

My eyes flickered across to the window seat on the other side.

"I like to ride on the right," she explained.

I was going to argue? Mumbling something, I stood up and moved aside to let her get past me. Before she sat, she went to pull a blanket and a pillow from the overhead rack. As she stretched to reach, her sweater pulled out of her waistband. I was treated to the sight of a two-inch strip of her midriff, gleaming white, and the delicious indentation of her navel.

My cock reacted. I sat down quickly and hid it under my laptop. She snapped the light for our seats off and sat down.

"Writer?" the girl asked, looking at my screen. "Movie scripts, right?"

"Yeah. Trying."

"Me, too. Not writing. I'm an actress, heading for Hollywood."

"Me, too," I told her. "Hollywood. I'm Trent Porter."

She gave me her fingertips. "DeeDee Dahl. That's not my real name, of course. DeeDee for double-D—get it?" She pulled her shoulders back.

"Yes, I get it."

"I'm hoping to be typecast as a dumb blonde."

"But you're not." I managed not to make it a question.

"Master's degree in literature, bachelor's in drama."

"Wow."

"So, who do you know?"

I gave her my very best and sexiest completely blank look.

"Any contacts in Hollywood?"

Ahh. "No."

"Me either. We must be mad, right?"

At least she was still talking to me. "Time will tell."

She asked me, "If I take a nap, will it disturb you?"

I told her it wouldn't, though having her anywhere within a hundred miles disturbed me. After all, her incredible left leg was less than three inches from my right one. She slumped back, pushing her feet forward. Her skirt worked higher. DeeDee rested her pillow on the window and her cheek on her pillow. As she half-turned away from me, the back of her calf pressed against my knee. She pulled her blanket over herself and settled down, leaving me wide awake with an erection Tarzan and three of his apes could have swung on.

I sat there, very aware of every breath she took, every slight movement of her pornographic body. After about twenty minutes, she half turned in her sleep and pulled her knees up. Her bottom pressed against my thigh. I swear her pussy was radiating heat at me.

Eventually my hard-on softened. Then she got restless, wriggling and arching in her sleep. DeeDee swung round with her eyes closed and flopped her head down on my shoulder. Her right hand landed on my thigh. She began to snore softly.

Against my strict orders, my cock grew again. Embarrassed that someone would notice, I tugged the end of DeeDee's blanket over my lap. Eventually, I must have dozed off. I woke with DeeDee's face still nestled into my shoulder, my arm around her, and, eureka, her hand still on my thigh and very close to my ever-stiffening cock.

What if I slowly moved my leg away? Or very gently took her by her wrist and . . .

DeeDee said, "It's two more days to LA. It could get very boring, couldn't it."

I made a noise of agreement.

"We could entertain each other," she suggested.

I croaked, "How?"

"We could make out."

"For two days?" I looked around. The bus was mostly dark, with just a couple of seats near the front lit up. "What about the other people?"

DeeDee giggled and squeezed my thigh. "I don't want to make out with them."

Again, I managed a realistic blank stare.

"Just kidding. No one can see us, can they? We could make out at night and nap by day. Anyway, lots of couples kiss and cuddle on buses." She licked her lips with the tip of her pink tongue. "And we've got a blanket."

I didn't think she meant us to put the blanket over our heads so I guessed that she intended to do more than just kissing.

I said, "Um," and that was all I got out because those pouty lips of hers rose up to meet mine.

Her mouth was sweet, with a trace of peppermint that had me thinking she'd popped one while I slept. I made it mainly a lip-kiss and pulled back before it got serious.

"Can you spare a mint?" Ever the suave gentleman.

She produced a pack from somewhere under the blanket and gave me half a dozen. "I've got more," she assured me. I wasn't reassured by getting six upfront and the promise of more. Note to self, when sitting near a hot chick on a long bus ride, don't eat onion rings with your burger.

Clearly my quick wit and my exceptional personal hygiene

were winning her over. I crunched three and got back to her lips, feeling confident enough to make a thorough exploration of her mouth. DeeDee's tongue was very mobile. It trembled in her mouth and then in mine. It was pink with a pointy tip, not a flat tongue but one that seemed to have waves or valleys, though that could be because of the way it moved against my own tongue. I'd never known a tongue to show signs of being aroused before, but her tongue appeared to harden the more we kissed. We kissed and kissed and then kept on kissing until we were both breathless. I wondered if I dared make the next move but she decided for me. Her hand took mine and put it on her bare waist.

She whispered, "Enjoy."

I did. I enjoyed the slick-smooth skin of her waist and the elegantly sculpted contours of her rib cage. Then the backs of my fingers brushed the voluptuous undercurve of her right breast.

"My nipples," she confided, "are very sensitive."

Her sweater was tight. I had to sort of scrunch down to get my arm up under it and found the position pretty cramped, but that wasn't going to stop me. My fingertips found the crinkled peak and teased it into growing. I explored it, learning and memorizing its shape and texture and springiness. DeeDee's lips trailed from my neck to my mouth. She panted minty breath. Her tongue was fierce and wet and sweet. I rolled her nipple, gradually applying more pressure.

She gasped, "Yes," into my mouth.

A cramp seized my hand. Fuck. It hurt like a son of a bitch, but somehow I fought it and managed to keep toying with her now engorged tidbit.

The bus lurched and sighed. I peered past DeeDee's curls and out the window. Dark buildings flashed by. A crack of pink lit the horizon. We'd come off the highway.

"We're stopping," I told DeeDee.

"For now," she said.

I worked my reluctant hand down and free. Somehow, I adjusted my cock so that its head was trapped behind the buckle of my belt.

It was a two-hour stop. We ate Sausage Egg McMuffins and parted to get showered and changed. She'd suggested that the first one ready would get back on the bus to hold our seats. I got back first and waited impatiently, irrationally fearing that she'd somehow disappear. When she showed, she looked so good it was like a shock to my system. She was in denim, a zipped bomber jacket that came down to a band just under her chest and a skirt that covered her from three inches below her navel to the tops of her thighs.

It was morning light by now and so we were on hiatus from our nighttime activities.

I spent the day in a fever. I couldn't work and I couldn't nap. My balls were tight and my cock hard. All I could think about was how long it was until dark. Why the hell couldn't we meet and travel together in December? Or during thunderstorm season when the day never really ever seemed to begin? But no, it was sunny skies all the way and I, for one, was miserable. DeeDee read trashy mags and nodded off from time to time. Once in a while, my fingers brushed her thigh or hers touched mine and my cock jumped inside my jeans.

At seven that evening, when we got back on board after the dinner break, she told me, "Sunset's a little after eight. You doing anything at about twenty minutes later?"

I nodded because I couldn't speak. At eight, DeeDee got the blanket and pillow down and turned off the light. I put my hand on her leg under the blanket and amused myself by stroking gently while we waited for dark. Twenty minutes later or so Dee-Dee turned into my arms and pulled the blanket up to our throats. "Remember where you were?" she said huskily. Her jacket's zipper rasped.

I had no trouble remembering and my hand wasn't in danger of cramping because of the easier access and new angle. I cupped and squeezed her breast and tried its weight in my palm but I knew what she wanted and didn't make her wait too long.

A nipple is a simple thing but with so many possibilities. I stroked and rolled and tugged and flickered my fingertips on its tip. Dee-Dee made little noises in her throat. When I'd pinched and pulled her right nipple until it had to be tender, I switched to her left.

She writhed and shuddered. "I wish we were alone, so you could suck on it," she said.

"Me, too."

Her hand reached up to her shoulder where I held her, and pulled on my wrist. Clever girl! Now both my hands were active on each of her breasts. However, it turned out that she had something else in mind entirely.

"I'm not wearing any panties."

"Oh." Clearly I intended to wow Hollywood with my gripping dialogue.

My left hand dropped to her thigh, then stroked upward. Her thighs parted. My fingers found the wet heat and the folds of sweet flesh. While still kissing, my right hand kept kneading her tit, and my left explored inside.

"Clit," she said.

I'd never known a girl who'd boldly tell me what she wanted me to do before. She wanted her clit played with? I was game.

Fingering her clit and her nipple and sucking on her tongue had me so horny I could scream, but my first priority was her pleasure. My thumb was rhythmically compressing the nub between her pussy's lips when DeeDee jerked in my arms and subsided with a sigh and a breathy, "Thank you."

"My pleasure." And I meant it.

I just held her for a while. My hand stroked her hair. My lips brushed her temple. It was self-control of heroic proportions because I was about to explode in my jeans.

Eventually she pecked the corner of my mouth and told me, "Your turn."

She should be a writer. I'd never heard sweeter words.

She unbuckled my belt. Her fingers tugged my zipper down, delved into my jeans, found my stiffy, and worked it out. I held my breath. Whatever she planned to do with my cock, it was fine by me. To my surprise, she stood up and peered over the back of the seats in front of us.

"There's no one in the back half of the bus. Move over to the window seat."

Covering myself with the blanket as best I could, despite her assurance that we couldn't be seen, I slid over. DeeDee turned to face the aisle, lifted her brief skirt, and sat on my lap, impaling herself. My cock sank into scalding wetness, which was delightful, but how the fuck was I to fuck her like that?

"Keep still," she said. "Play with my tits some more. Please, Trent."

So I did. Under the cover of the blanket, I tweaked and tugged and tweaked some more. DeeDee wriggled on my cock. Her internal muscles squeezed it. Once in a while, her hips rotated. Her kisses became frantic once more. She was getting excited again. I was still there from before, and getting more and more desperate. There was no way I was going to come since she couldn't really move much. It was too subtle to push me over the edge, but enough to keep me in an extreme state of arousal. I was trying to figure out how to maneuver her or me or both of us so that I could get some traction when she dropped a hand between her own thighs and frigged herself to her second orgasm. Her internal muscles clenched on me.

"I . . ." I tried to say.

"I know," she said. DeeDee lifted off my cock and slithered off my lap. Her legs were under the seat in front of us, her arms resting on either side of my thighs, and her head, her blond, curly, adorable head with the pouty lips and amazing tongue was face to cock with me. She pulled the blanket over her head, wrapped her hand about my still wet cock, then slowly, sweetly, perfectly closed that fabulous mouth over the head.

My legs spread and stiffened. I felt under the blanket to trace my finger along her lips, where they were stretched around my shaft. Her right hand continued to pump me. Her left tickled my balls. After what I'd endured that night, it was no surprise that I flooded her mouth in about two minutes flat.

She emerged licking her lips and climbed back onto the seat. "Try to get a little sleep now," she said. "I promise I'll wake you in time for a quickie before dawn."

And she did. She woke me with a slow handjob. I returned the compliment with my fingers back on her clit and she came twice before I came the once, but I wasn't about to object.

I spent the next day horny but not desperate. I even got some work done. DeeDee read to me from her tabloids, bringing me up to date on which stars were anorexic and which ones were gay and which incredibly handsome male superstars had been caught rutting with pig-faced prostitutes.

We touched once in a while. She teased me by asking me how I'd enjoyed having my cock in her mouth and things like that. Over our fast-food meals, we shared our dreams. Evening came, and night, and we snuggled under our blanket. She'd kept the same jacket and skirt on, because it gave me easier access to her body. She told me that without blushing. Her fingers stroked my cock. Mine played with her pussy and her nips. Our tongues were old friends.

About one in the morning, DeeDee stood up again. I expected her back on my lap but she sidled out into the aisle with a whispered, "Follow me."

She led me into one of the bus's two small toilets. Even though we were pressed together in the cramped quarters, she managed to squat, pulling my jeans and boxers down with her. Her mouth did wonderful things to my cock and I felt I was getting close when she wriggled back up and hitched her bottom onto the tiny counter. Her legs spread wide.

"Fuck me, Trent."

She was buttery-soft inside, but firm enough to grip me tightly. Her hands clasped the back of my neck and pulled my face down to her breast. "Suck my tit, Trent," she said. "I've wanted you to do that since the moment we met."

So I sucked and fucked and she diddled herself. Again, she came twice to my once, which was fine. We made our way back to our seats and spent most of the night contentedly kissing and cuddling. Just before dawn, she slipped her hand back to my cock, and jerked me off, catching my come in a Wendy's napkin.

At four in the afternoon we pulled into the bus station in LA.

"Do you have a cell phone number?" I asked. "Or an address?"

DeeDee gave me a sad smile and slowly shook her head. "It's been great fun, Trent," she said. "I've really enjoyed our trip together but this is where our new lives start. From here on, I'm a starlet and you're a writer. I know I plan to play dumb blondes but there isn't a blonde in Hollywood so dumb she'd fuck a writer."

And she was gone.

Isaac Andrews

*Welcome to Pasadena, home of the Rose Parade, the Rose
Bowl, and raunchy, nasty sex with big, aggressive men
and lonely, ignored housewives.*

Like Chinese Food

I left my husband, Cooper, on the fifth of the month. I hadn't
slept with him for six weeks. By the fifteenth I was horny enough
for an intimate relationship with a doorknob. To be honest, I'd
tried it. The strain of the position made for an interesting but
not very satisfying encounter. The damned thing was all circum-
ference and no length.

Thick is nice, but I needed *long* and *warm*. There were any
number of gentlemen of my acquaintance who would have been
delighted to spend an afternoon between my thighs but with my
divorce pending I had to be discreet. In any case, it wasn't a
gentleman I needed. After years of gentle, I needed rough.

I hopped a plane to Pasadena and booked into the Excelsior.
By the time I'd unpacked it was eight in the evening. For
Pasadena that was pretty late, so I showered without masturbating, made up, slipped into some sexy undies and a cute little
dress, and set off to hunt myself a man.

As I closed my suite's door, a gorgeous hunk in working
clothes came out of the suite next to mine.

"Are you from room service?" I asked.

"No, ma'am. Maintenance. Been fixing the air conditioner."

I did an about-turn and called the front desk to complain
about my air conditioner. That hunk was at my door ten minutes later. I followed close behind him as he went to my cooling
unit. When he squatted, his pants stretched tight across an ass
that looked like a split boulder. I checked how hard his buns

were by standing close enough behind him that my legs pressed on them.

He said, "I don't see nothing wrong." As he stood, with me so close, his body slid up mine.

Looking straight at his throat, I murmured, "But I'm so hot." I swayed to drag my breasts across his shirt. "What do you think it could be?"

He grinned. "I'd say you was running a fever, lady."

"You think?" I laid my hand over the bulge in his pants and gave it a squeeze. "I do have a fever, something awful. Do you have anything to fix that?"

"What you got in mind, lady?"

I touched a finger to my neck. "You could start with some lip-service right about here."

His beard was rough but his lips were soft and his tongue was very wet and energetic. As he nuzzled, I reached behind and unzipped my dress.

"You in a rush?" he asked.

"I haven't had intercourse for over a month, so yes, I am."

He frowned. "Intercourse?"

It seemed that he didn't understand polite language. I could live with that. I undid the buttons of his shirt, looked into his eyes, and told him, "I haven't been fucked in an age. I need a cock. You've got one. Am I making myself clear?"

"Clear as day, lady. You want to go slum-fucking with a rough stud, right? And I'm elected?"

"Bright boy!"

He turned me and wrapped his powerful arms around me. His fingers freed my tits from my bra. Callused thumbs worked my nipples. "This what you want?"

In answer, I reached back and yanked his fly zipper down. My hand worked inside and found a firm length of hot, throbbing cock, already nice and stiff. I pulled it out and ran my fingers along it.

"Like it?" he asked.

"So far. Do my tits harder. Fuck. Like this." I reached up, grasping my own tender nubs in my fingers and pinched and pulled them, sending electric shocks all the way to my clit. I then wrapped my hands around my pale, heavy breasts and kneaded them like dough.

"A real lady, huh? Like this?" His fingers clamped on my nipples, twisted them, and pinched their tips.

"On the bed," I panted. "Get naked. I want to see you."

He stripped and threw himself onto his back. I straddled him and took a closer look at his cock. It was all of nine inches and was already leaking. I fisted his skin down tight, leaned over and lapped the clear pearl from the eye of his cock.

His fist knotted in my hair and pushed my face down. That was exactly what I wanted: rough. His cock rammed between my lips, all the way to the back of my throat. The best I could, I sucked on it and ran my tongue up its underside. He was crude but he wasn't selfish. His thick fingers pushed the crotch of my panties aside. Two of them worked into me, deep and hard. He wasn't ignorant, either. Their pads rubbed on my G-spot while the ball of his thumb pressed on my clit. With my being so needy, I had an instant orgasm.

"You come easy, lady," he told me.

I slurped off his cock. "And often. Get your tongue in there and I'll show you."

His palm cracked down on my bottom. I yelped. "What was that for?!"

"You want it rough, lady? That means you do like you're told and don't give no fucking orders!"

In my meekest voice, quivering with excitement, I murmured, "Sorry. Of course. Whatever you say."

"So take hold of my cock and rub it on your tongue, bitch! I'm gonna have some fun with this cunt of yours."

I wrapped a fist around his shaft, extended the flat of my tongue, and rubbed. His fingers explored me, slipping in and out of my cunt, then withdrew. Oh! Thumbs now, both of them, one at the top of my slit and the other at the bottom, stretched me out long so that my cunt lips came together. His strong tongue probed between them.

"Tickle my balls," he said.

I scratched gently. His thumbs opened me wide.

"Nice in there, lady. All wet and pink and purple."

Showing off, I flexed my internal muscles.

"That was neat. Do it again."

I obliged and pursed my lips on the eye of his cock. My mouth made spit. My tongue smeared that over his cock's head and then I sucked it back into my mouth.

"You're good, lady. That was nice. I think you earned a souvenir."

His face nuzzled deep along my mons. His lips nibbled, then started sucking. It was gentle at first, then harder.

"What you doing?" I asked.

"Never got a hickey before?"

"Not there."

"Well, you are now." His mouth worked again, so hard I could feel my blood coming to the surface of my skin. "There," he said finally, "Now you got a mark to remember me by, where nobody but you'n me knows where it is. Do that thing with spit again."

I went back to work on his tasty cock but it was hard to concentrate. He was using his thumbs again but this time one was pressing on the rosebud of my ass. Thank fuck he'd wet it with my juices, 'cause it was working its way slowly past the tight ring of muscle and actually inside.

I moaned, "No! Not there! I've never . . . Ouch!"

He'd slapped me again. Well, I'd asked for rough and he was delivering. I tried to relax my ass but it kept clenching on his thumb.

"Better let me in," he warned. "I'm being nice. Some guys'd just fuck your ass without loosening you up first."

"Fuck my ass?" I gasped.

"Cunt first, though. That way I'll last longer in your ass."

"No one has ever . . . oh! Oh fuck! That feels so good."

"Yeah—for me, too. Like this?" His thumb worked in and out a few times, withdrew completely, then pushed in again.

I came.

"I see you do," he said. "Okay, bitch. On your back. I'm gonna fuck you now."

The bastard heaved me onto my back and climbed over me. He had me pinned, his shins on my knees, pressing them apart so wide my thighs hurt. His hand held my wrists above my head. Looking down at me, he said, "Stick your tongue out, lady, where I can get a taste of it whenever I like."

I obeyed, of course. I had no choice and didn't want one. This was exactly what I'd flown to Pasadena to find. He reached down, took hold of his cock, and guided its head between my cunt's sopping lips. As he leaned forward, his shaft pressed on my clit.

"You wanna get off? You better fuck up at me then."

What I wanted was his cock buried deep in me but he was in charge. I did my best to hump up at him. His face came down, bringing his lips to my stretched-out tongue. He sucked it so hard its roots ached. Holding still, making me do all the fucking, he drew on my tongue and twisted my left nipple between cruel fingers. Thrills shot through me, from tongue to nipple to clit. The strain on my thighs was agony and that just spurred me on. I wanted to tell him I was on the point of coming, but my tongue was trapped. My face screwed up. Convulsions started deep inside me. My belly clenched. My orgasm was so close, closer . . . oh fuck! It burst!

That fucking bastard must have sensed it. As my climax gushed, he thrust, flattening me. His cock pistoned deep inside me, forcing my own flood back into my womb. It was incredible! I rode on wave after wave of cataclysmic orgasms. Somewhere in the middle of that pounding ecstasy, I felt his scalding flood. My coming had triggered his.

He flopped off me, gasping.

"That was nice," I told him. "Thanks. You can go now."

"Like fuck."

"What do you mean?"

"I told you. Your ass is next."

I wriggled away from him. My ass clenched at the thought of his massive cock. "No—that's okay. Another time, maybe?"

"Now." He tugged me toward him.

"If you think I'm going to kneel and let you—"

He reared up over me, lifting both of my ankles, spread wide. "You've never been ass-fucked before," he said with a grin. "You think I want you kneeling? No fucking way! I want to watch your eyes as I do it." He lifted me and walked forward on his knees. His hands folded my knees to my tits. He held both my ankles above my head in one huge fist.

"No!" I wriggled but he had me totally, deliciously, helpless.

He leaned forward, resting his chest on my calves. I felt his knob nuzzle my ring.

"Please, no?"

He pushed. My sphincter parted. Oh fuck, it was incredible! I'd never felt so controlled and so violated. The pressure increased. Slowly, inexorably, that mighty weapon forced its way into my most forbidden place. I felt so dirty, so humiliated.

Grinning down at me, he said, "You love it, don't you?"

I nodded. By then, perspiration poured between my breasts. My cunt was juiced again. I could feel the trickle into the crease of my ass. He leaned harder, driving slowly deeper. When he was in so far there was no farther he could go, he rocked on me, see-sawing my ass under him. The thumb of his free hand squished my clit, crushing it against my pubic bone. As he rubbed on it and worked his cock in my behind, I came again. Fluids gushed from me. His balls slapped the base of my spine. I could hardly breathe. I felt stuffed, impaled. No man had ever dominated me like that, taking me over, using me.

He began to bounce up and down, sliding in and out. Once he pulled all the way from me. The suction of my ass was so intense it felt like he was turning me inside out.

"Put it back," I begged. "I can come again, honest."

"Then come for me, slut!"

His crude words ignited me. Folded as I was, movement was almost impossible, but somehow I managed to curl tighter, moving his cock in me.

He left my clit to work my nipples again, then dipped his fingers into my cunt and made me suck my own come off them. Each new trick he taught me made me climax again. At long last, he pulled back, almost out of me, and drove hard and deep, squirting his jism far inside.

That time, after falling off me, he just marched off to the bathroom, then reappeared wiping the sweat off his chest. "Nice, lady. Any time you need cooling, just call maintenance." And he was gone.

I lay panting for a while and then checked the bedside clock. Midnight. Too late to go out and see the sights, such as they were. I went to the bathroom and cleaned up. On the way back to my bed I heard a noise in the corridor outside. I cracked the door and peered through. It was a youngish guy in a waiter's outfit, backing out of the room opposite. Hmmm. Nice buns.

"You room service?" I asked.

"Yes, ma'am."

"Must be busy, working the whole hotel."

"I just serve two floors, ma'am. This one and seven. It's pretty quiet most nights."

"Really?" I opened the door just enough to give him a look at one leg.

He looked, went red, and licked his lips. Good. He wasn't gay. Some waiters are.

"Night, ma'am."

"Night." I closed my door and slipped into a short robe before picking up the phone. "Room service? Can I get a platter of sandwiches and a magnum of champagne? Thanks."

Like I said, before the maintenance man it'd been a long time since I'd had a good fuck. To me, men are like Chinese food. After an hour, you're hungry for more, you know?

Nancy Delp

JennaTip #9: Being a Dirty Girl

Sometimes you just want messy, filthy, obscene, depraved sex. Earlier we discussed shaved, clean, nice-smelling guys. But there are times you may just want him sweaty and dirty and smelly. It's okay to like it both ways. Variety is the spice of life, after all. If you want to smell his spunky junk and feel nasty and naughty, then go for it.

Other than saying "deeper" and "harder," sometimes it's okay to want to say "hurt me." Now, you might not want to be really injured, but there is a very fine line between pleasure and pain and combining the two can be a huge erotic release and turn on.

If you know what you want, know your limits, and have a great partner who has control, why not have some hard, slammin' sex and get really sweaty and dirty?

So grab a handful of hair, smear your lipstick, tear your clothes, come everywhere, and roll in it like a pig in mud. Sure, clean is nice but dirty is filthy and maybe tonight you'd like to have some fabulously filthy sex.

For example, there's this woman who was having an affair with a guy she worked with and she had him come on her face and neck and then she let it dry and walked around the whole day with it still on her. They were both totally hot for each other the whole day and had to pretend they didn't like each other because the office didn't allow dating between employees. It was dirty. It was messy. And it was totally hot!

Try a big, meaty man sandwich with a cool bit of sweetness between!

Double the Meat

The smell of stale cigarette smoke, sweat, and dried sperm hit my face as soon as the motel room's door opened. The shades were drawn and the light fixture had dim bulbs, probably to hide the garage-sale furnishings. This $40-a-night special wasn't good for anything but truck drivers and fucking.

Ed walked in first. His dirty blond hair was cropped so short it could have passed for chin stubble. He'd replaced any need for a shirt with his inch-thick tattoos. Even though he was thin, he was muscled and tight.

Brad, behind me, was too eager. He'd spent the ride here stroking my thighs and knee-high black leather boots. As soon as I'd gotten out of the car he'd reached up my skirt and grabbed my bare ass with one hand and wrapped my brown hair up in the other. He didn't let go until he turned around to close the motel room door behind us.

For that, I'd make him wait.

Ed was looking at me now. Half his top lip was swollen and the welt on his right cheek was fast darkening into a black eye. He moved against me until his palms rested against my nipples, scuffing them through my T-shirt. Brad began working his hands on my ass again and I was getting horny sandwiched between them.

"Who's first?" Ed asked.

Brad pushed Ed's shoulder away. "I am," he claimed as they squeezed me aside and, after making fists, bounced their chests against each other.

Brad's face had fared better than Ed's, with a small cut above the eye, already healing, and a slightly swollen jaw. But the fingers of his right punching hand were swollen and brittle. He was bigger than Ed, his hair was dark, and it looked as though it was chiseled into his head. I let the two hiss at each other a while before I pulled my skirt off and handed it to Brad.

"Ed's first. You wait," I demanded.

"Yeah, why don't you go get us some beer?" Ed didn't wait for Brad's "Fuck you" before he buried my lips in his. I didn't always kiss with my eyes shut, but I couldn't stand the bruises on Ed's face. He wiggled my shirt up to my neck, but stopped and moaned quietly as I unscrambled his belt and fly. His pants dropped and I cupped his balls in my palms. He was already hard, and dribbles of precome dropped onto my wrists as I pushed him back to sit on the bed.

His cock was thick, long, and without tattoos. I pulled off the rest of my shirt, then his sneakers and pants and, kissing him hard on the forehead, forced him back onto the bed. My lips moved to the head of his prick. I couldn't really see Brad, though occasionally I glimpsed his shadow as he paced back and forth behind me. My mouth worked on Ed's dick as he eased back on the bed and laid his palms up in a posture of bedroom surrender.

Once I'd had him convinced that he'd get an easy orgasm down my throat, I mounted his face, his arms on the front of my thighs, my ass waving at his stranded dick. I still had my boots on and this didn't seem to bother Ed at all. If I was hurting his bruised face he didn't complain and I didn't care as I worked his tongue like a silk vibrator.

Brad wasn't able to just stand by and wait his turn. He'd undressed and while I rode Ed's face, he leaned in and grabbed my breasts. I noticed a string of bruises along Brad's side, running from his underarm to the bottom of his ribs. Ed punched at him, but as my thighs were holding his upper body captive, there was no power in it. Brad retreated, punched back, and then moved in again. Soon Ed's attention was back to his tongue and Brad was alternately massaging and licking at my nipples. I felt Ed's lower body bucking as he came, unassisted, all over his own stomach. And this triggered my own brief but intense orgasm.

"My turn," Brad insisted before my thighs were able to relax. He was stronger than I thought, and lifted me up and off Ed's face with ease. Then he laid me on the bed so that the back of my head rested in the puddle of jism on Ed's stomach. My legs weren't fully spread before Brad's thick dick was in me. Just the thought of my fluids mixing with another man's drool and yet another man's semen sent me into a long, sustained orgasm where my moans almost shook the room's cheap wallpaper free.

Brad's hand scooped under my ass and cupped my cheeks as Ed took over, teasing my breasts with his fingers. There wasn't much style to Brad's fucking; his thrusts were uneven, more wild than passionate. I play-kicked at the bruises on his chest with the heel of my boot, which made him smile. Then I wrapped my legs around his waist and guided his thrusts until his back straightened and our mouths opened in silent screams. My ass quivered and he came deep inside me. Ed scooped up some of his come from his belly and rubbed it onto my nipples. Marking me. My body responded with another orgasm that made my neck buck and my fingers dig into the mattress. I felt our juices dripping from my pussy and onto the bed.

A moment later, our heads were on the pillows, with me set in the middle. Occasionally, between kissing me and exploring my body with their fingers, they would chat.

"Fuck you," Ed would say.

"Asshole," Brad would counter.

Brad would punch Ed square in the shoulder. Ed would slap

Brad's chest with the heel of his palm. Neither of them were going to show or tell if the blows hurt.

I knew this would go on for hours. These guys were going to punch at each other, stopping occasionally to fuck me when their hard-ons got in the way. It was my fault, of course. We were strangers just a couple hours ago when we met at the fight club. It was my idea to offer myself as a prize. And I wasn't a lady about it either.

"I'll fuck the winner," I said in front of a room full of people. Then they had to go and tie.

Stephen Todd

JennaTip #10: Threesomes

When three people have sex together, it's a threesome. Duh. You know.

There are a lot of different ways for a threesome to work out, however. If you suggest a threesome to your guy, he, like most guys, will be all for it, thinking you want to invite the hot-wings girl to come home with you. It's mostly what's depicted in movies and magazines. However, just like in this story, a threesome can happen with one girl and two guys or three girls or three guys. However, for it really to be a threesome all three people should be having sex all together and not taking turns.

Of course, there are a variety of ways that two men can fuck a woman at once. For penetrating positions (ones where the cocks are entering her), they can sandwich her and double-penetrate (one cock in her ass and one in her pussy), or create a spit roast or Chinese fingercuffs (where one cock is in her mouth and the other is either in her ass or pussy in the typical doggy-style position).

For nonpenetrating positions, there are hand jobs, oral sex, caressing and touching, and the like.

As with everything involving other people, be open, honest, and really understand why you want to do this and what the possible impact might be on your relationship, if you are in one. If you aren't and this is kind of a free-for-all, then just be safe and have a ball, or two balls.

Remember, when someone does you a real service, tip generously!

Hostile Takeover

Maxine was at the hotel's front desk. Cute girl. Young and professional. I gave her a wink, and she waved me on to the elevator.

Riding up, I tightened the belt around my trench coat and patted down my short, near-blond hair. I wasn't an overly attractive woman. Big glasses, small breasts, short legs. But, over the years, I'd learned a lot about the rich guys who called for my services. Number one rule: they either wanted to be making money, or spending it.

Right on time I slapped the door of Suite 716. And right on time, F.L. answered my hard knock. He was younger than I thought, not even thirty. Slender for a man, with thin arms and a boyish pout on his lips. He was only wearing the small, black blindfold that I sent him along with a dozen roses and my simple instructions. First, put the flowers in water. Second, wear nothing but the blindfold. Last, place ten crisp Benjamins on a table near the door.

I could see the table when I stepped in. On it was a vase full of yellow roses and a short stack of hundred-dollar bills.

This bad boy knew how to follow instructions.

"Is that you, Andrea?" He whispered so softly that I had to guess at the words.

He winced as I carved my initials into his chest with the tips of my nails.

"You only speak when spoken to," I told him. "You address me as Mistress Andrea or Mistress. Your choice. Your only choice."

He swallowed. So hard I could hear his throat click. I locked the door and dropped my trench coat. I wasn't exactly dressed for the office. A black leather corset pushed my bare breasts up and out, my nipples spilling over the top. My matching fishnet stockings were topped off with lacy garters. The silk of my black thong brushed my delicate parts as I began to circle him like a predator.

I spied into the suite and saw a small room with a wet bar and couch immediately ahead.

"Kneel on the floor in front of the couch, and do it immediately," I demanded.

The blindfold made it tough for him to obey but he tried, and I appreciated it. In fact, he smacked face-first into a wall. Then he stumbled on a carpet wrinkle and banged his shin on a corner of the coffee table. He eventually found the floor in front of the couch, kneeled down, and draped one arm onto the sofa cushions.

I looked around for something personal and saw a financial newspaper folded on top of the bar. Perfect. I glanced at the stock market report. Saw that Eramasing Corp had been circled with a sloppy pen. Then I rolled the paper into a log and moved over to Mr. F.L.

"Off the couch." I slapped him on the arm with the newspaper. It couldn't have hurt much. But the sound was amplified and I'm sure it was a shock.

"Yes, Mistress." His arm hastily dropped to his side.

I poked his leg with the tip of my boot, and he whimpered. Too many hours spent in an office gave him a hunched-over look. I poked him again until his hands were on his thighs.

I sat down on the couch and crossed my legs. "Hands behind your back!" I ordered and he quickly complied.

"Kiss my knee." I knew he'd have a hard time finding it. I smacked him on the forehead with the newspaper.

"Ouch," he whined. So I smacked him again across the mouth.

"It didn't hurt, you pussy." And that gave me another reason to puppy-slap him. Eventually he got there and started licking my knee through the nylons. I tapped the newspaper across his temple again.

"I said kiss. Not lick."

"Yes, Mistress." His head bounced back before he brought his lips forward again and planted a sweet pucker on my knee.

"You seem distracted." Not totally in character, but I had a point I was trying to make.

"I do?" He was concerned, nearly to the point of panic.

"You've got something heavy on your mind."

"Nothing, Mistress," he lied.

"I want to get back to our business. But I don't want you being half-assed about it. Tell me what's going on." I was back in my role. But I don't think he noticed the changes.

"I," he began, then stopped short. Hands still behind his back, he sat his ass down on the carpet. "Have a big deal going tomorrow."

Here it was. These business guys couldn't help it. Once they started, they couldn't shut up.

"I'm the major shareholder in a blue-chip company. But I want a controlling share. The prices are way up there. Tomorrow I bring them down, drop the stock price by at least thirty percent, and grab a majority share cheap." He started laughing. A sinister, sick laugh.

It was his most appealing quality out of few.

"How do you drop the price?" I asked. Then I added innocently, "I'm not good with math and numbers."

He hesitated. Didn't want to answer. So I used the paper to slap him right in the chest. That got his attention. Made him an easy target.

"I set up false reports. Went out late today to the market, media, and bloggers. They say a Chinese company just announced a competing brand. Cheaper. Faster. They'll report it as rumors first. Prices will plummet. By the time it's figured out that it's just a rumor with no truth behind it, I'll own most of the company." F.L. laughed again, but this time, more to himself.

"What if the stock doesn't recover?" I asked, just to torment him.

He stopped breathing. Then said, "Of course it will go back up. The rumors will be proven to be just rumors. They're just realistic enough to have a short-term impact, but not realistic enough to pass muster. That's the way it works."

"As long as it isn't the Eramasing Corp.," I said, watching for telltale signs that would give me the answer I wanted.

He probably thought he was playing cool, but his sudden freeze and quick intake of breath gave him away.

"Why do you say that?" His voice shook slightly.

"I hear they're going to be investigated. Some kind of auntie trustee thing? I hear rumors from the other women."

"An antitrust suit? Where did they hear that?" He was trying to reverse the roles. Plugging me for answers.

"From some military guy. A general, I think." I smacked the coffee table with the paper. The sound made his shoulders rise and chin sink.

"A general?" His face became scrunched up. Like he was confused.

"The attorney general. Whoever that is," I paused, allowing the words to settle in his head. Then I slapped him with the paper again. "Enough shop talk. Get back to work, slave boy."

"Yes, Mistress." He seemed glad to change the subject.

I watched him lick his lips. That seemed like a good way to start. I spread my legs, hooked my right ankle over his shoulder.

Pulled him close. Close enough so he could smell my scent. His nostrils quivered and he bit his lip. Like a good boy, he awaited my instruction.

"Does the slave boy want to please me?"

"Yes," he whispered.

I grabbed him by the hair, pulled him even closer. His mouth was practically on top of my pussy. I touched myself, then wiped my wet fingers on his upper lip. He whimpered with pleasure.

"Lick me, slave." I slapped the back of his head with the newspaper. "Make it good. Don't stop until I tell you. Don't come until I say it's okay."

He pressed his lips against me, tasting me, licking me all over. I gave him an A for effort, but he had a lot to learn.

I swiped the back of his head with the newspaper. "Use your tongue like a cock, slave. I don't feel a damn thing yet." I was lying, but I wanted him to work for it.

I kept tapping him with the newspaper while giving him directions. "Lick my clit. Lower. Fuck me with your tongue."

He licked me with more effort. Sucking my clit into his mouth, working his tongue into my deep folds. I sighed and rested my boots on his lower back.

"That's it. Suck my pussy. Make me come."

He moaned, needing to come, almost trembling from the effort to hold back. My thighs grabbed him by the ears and pressed him against me. I fucked his mouth, using my clit like a cock, smashing his mouth with my pussy. I came all over his lips and chin, drenching his face.

I dropped back on the couch and said, "Come for me, bitch."

He spasmed, losing his balance and falling back on his heels. His cock shot straight up, spurting come all over his stomach and thighs.

He was done after that. But I still had more work to do. I instructed that he could only take the blindfold off after I was gone. Then I took my thousand in cash, and left.

On the elevator down, I began punching numbers on my cell phone, needing to shift funds around. There was a blue-chip company out there with stock values about to dive and the prime player interested in grabbing up the stock now not so interested. If I set myself up right, when it recovered, my profit would be in the seven figures. Probably even higher.

Maxine, smiling, was still at the desk when I returned to the lobby area. She knew. Like all the hotel concierges in the city, she knew I was the one to call when an upper-level corporate type needed some relief. I dropped the ten Benjamins on the front desk and her eyes widened, then glowed.

It was a lot of money for Maxine, but pocket change to me.

O. Preston Telford

There is no such thing as too rich or too many shoes or too many eager hands up your skirt.

Goody Two-Shoes

You're absolutely right, darling, these sling-back pumps are by Prada, and yes, those cute strappy sandals I was wearing yesterday are by Manolo Blahnik. You must be wondering about my changed attitude to footwear, right? After all, only a year ago I was buying maybe three pair a year, tops, usually from Shoe Mart or Payless. Now it's a pair or two of top designer shoes or boots every single month. That's a radical change, right? Well, it all started last October.

The day had started soft and warm but by evening it was turning hard and gritty. Wet splotches were appearing on the sidewalk, threatening to turn into a major rainstorm. I needed a cab, fast, but every taxi in sight already had a snug and smug passenger or two. I lengthened my stride. Things got worse. My heel caught in a grating and snapped clean off. Luckily, there was a shoe store not a hundred yards farther on. I wasn't going to lurch and hobble my way along a busy street, so I jerked my heel free, took my shoes off, put them in my bag, and hurried on in my stocking feet. Each step I took, I felt a fresh run creep up the legs of my poor pantyhose.

My watch warned me that it was four minutes to six, which is closing time for most stores here on Wednesdays. When I got to it, the store was still lit up. The door opened at my touch. Sighing my relief, I padded in, ruined stockings and all.

The store's long narrow interior walls were covered in dove-gray watered silk. The mirrors were beveled and tinted pink. The carpet under my feet looked and felt like blond mink. The

Muzak was Mozart. I could smell Chanel No. 5. I got that I-don't-belong-here feeling, but I had no choice. New shoes were a necessity. I looked around and saw no one. I coughed. No one came. Somewhat nervous, I wandered along the displays. As I approached the far end I discovered that the store was L-shaped. I turned the corner but I still saw no one. I cleared my throat. That didn't work, so I coughed again, loudly.

Two pretty girls hurried from an archway that looked like it led to the storage area. It seemed that the store's employees wore uniforms: high-heeled black pumps, black hose, very short black flared skirts, white man-styled shirts, and men's ties, striped gray and pink.

I guess I'd caught them changing to go home or something. The girl with the black geometric-cut hair was fumbling to do up the buttons of her shirt. The blonde with flip-ups was tucking hers into her waistband. Both were flushed. Their lipstick was smudged.

"I'll help Madam, Fiona," the blonde said. "You go lock up."

"It's my turn," Fiona said. "You lock up, Darla."

I guessed that they were on commission, so I said, "You can both help me and split the sale."

"What a good idea! I'll be right back. Don't start without me." Darla made off toward the front of the store.

Fiona and I looked at each other and waited. Darla returned and said, "There! Now we won't be disturbed. Madam will have our full and undivided attention." She and Fiona exchanged looks that I didn't quite understand. Both nodded. They pulled up two of those stools with little ramps that shoe clerks use and produced foot-measuring sticks.

Darla said, "Your hose, Madam? You can't try shoes on with those on your feet, can you?"

Fiona added, "Will Madam remove them or should we?"

I blushed, stood up, and made a turn-your-backs twirling signal with one finger. They turned and so did I, for extra modesty, I suppose. Reaching up under one's skirt and tugging pantyhose down isn't an elegant operation at best. Mission accomplished, I balled my ruined garment and tucked it into my bag.

"You can turn round now," I told them.

They did, smirking. It was then that I noticed that there was a mirror on the far wall, so they could have watched me had they wanted to. The looks on their faces said that they had.

Somewhat bemused, I sat down on a deep bench seat that was upholstered in buttery leather. It felt soft enough to swallow me. As one, the girls sat on their stools, bent, and lifted my ankles. I sank deeper into the bench. It gave me a peculiar, almost helpless, feeling, that wasn't entirely unpleasant. My feet were measured thoroughly, length, width, even depth.

"Madam has lovely feet," Darla said.

"Thank you."

"Very pretty toes," Fiona added.

"Such elegant arches."

"And adorable insteps."

As each part of my foot was complimented, it was stroked by delicate fingertips. The effect was quite hypnotic and, I have to admit, sexually arousing.

"But chilled to the bone," Fiona said.

"We must warm them."

Their fingers cupped and massaged, kneaded and caressed. I leaned back, surrendering to the soothing sensations. Fiona held my instep against the smooth warmth of her young cheek. Darla planted a kiss at the base of my toes. Their attentions were becoming more and more intimate. I knew I should protest but delayed my objections for just one more second, then one more, and one more . . .

Darla's thumbs manipulated the tiny bones in the sole of the foot she held, while her lips closed around its big toe and sucked. Fiona knuckled the ball of my other foot while her warm wet tongue squirmed between its toes. My eyes closed, as if by not looking I could deny the reality of the sensuous liberties they were taking.

My feet were set down on the sloping ramps of their stools. I blinked.

"Hose," Fiona declared. "Madam must have hose."

Darla stood. "Black, of course."

"Of course." Fiona writhed erect.

"Style?"

"Madam must choose."

"We shall model for her." To me, Darla said, "Does Madam prefer this length?" She raised the hem of her short skirt to show me that her nylons ended midway up her smooth pale thighs, in three-inch bands of clinging lace.

"Or this?" Fiona continued. Her hose went all the way up to within an inch of the tops of her slender thighs and ended in thin black latex strips.

Both girls' skirts were held so high that I could see the glossy black satin that was stretched over their pubes. They waited, skirts raised, for my decision.

"Um—that length," I croaked, pointing to Darla's thighs.

"Excellent choice," they agreed. Fiona took her seat at my feet again. Darla disappeared and returned with a plastic package.

"These are from Leg Avenue," she told me. Her thumbnail slit the package. She pulled out a diaphanous stocking and handed it to Fiona. I moved to take it from her but Darla sat and they each lifted one of my feet into a lap, rendering me helpless to resist. The stockings were rolled down into little nylon nests.

My toes were inserted. Inch by leisurely inch, the stockings were rolled over my feet, fitted to my heels, and slowly smoothed up over my ankles and my calves. I tensed when four loving hands reached my knees. If I was going to protest, that would have been the time to do it, but my voice froze on me until it was too late. Delicate fingers were unrolling gossamer up my quivering thighs. It seemed that the lacy tops had to be adjusted and readjusted, with each pat and stroke sending little jolts of erotic electricity directly to my sex.

"There!" they said in unison. They tugged me to my feet.

"What?" I squeaked.

"You must model your stockings for us, just like we did ours for you," Fiona told me.

Until then, my part had been passive. I hadn't stopped them from touching me but neither had I actually done anything to actively participate. If I raised my skirt to show off my legs, I'd be encouraging them and be partly responsible for whatever followed. Did I dare?

"Fair's fair," Darla added.

Blushing furiously but not wanting to be a poor sport, I lifted the front of my skirt.

"Higher," Darla said.

"Much higher, please," Fiona coaxed.

I lifted my hem even farther.

"Oh dear," from Fiona.

Darla tutted.

"That will never do!"

Before I was even sure of their intent, they'd reached under my skirt and tugged my white cotton bikini briefs down to my ankles.

"What are you doing!?"

"You can't judge the appearance of shoes unless you are wearing hose," Darla explained.

Fiona tossed my undies aside. "And you can't judge the appearance of hose when you are wearing ugly panties."

"I—I—?"

"We don't sell lingerie," Darla told me. "When you replace those nasty things, we recommend thongs, preferably in black satin."

"Like ours," Fiona completed for her.

"But—" I protested.

"If you don't have any nice undies," I was informed, "it's better to go without than to wear ugly ones."

"But—" I tried again.

"If it makes Madam uncomfortable to have no panties on while we do," Fiona said, "voilà!"

Each girl reached up under her own short skirt and pulled down the tiny scrap of satin she'd been wearing with a flourish. I couldn't help but notice that Fiona's pubic hair had been reduced to a minute arrowhead of cropped fuzz, while Darla seemed to be totally bald there.

I stood, dumbstruck, simultaneously terrified and excited. I could have fled, barefoot and naked beneath my skirt. I should have fled and I would have fled, but perverse curiosity rooted me to the spot. If I'd left at that moment, I'd have wondered for the rest of my life what might have happened if I'd stayed.

So I stayed.

I was helped back into the bench seat. Darla fetched a pair of Salvatore Ferragamo ankle boots with rabbit-fur trim. No sooner had they been fitted to my feet than they were whisked away as not suiting me. Fiona brought out Dolce & Gabbana pumps that were decorated with vicious little metal spikes.

"Dita Von Teese would like these," Fiona told me.

"But they aren't for Madam, I don't think."

They produced a pair of Yves St. Laurent pumps, deceptively simple but cute, with kitten heels. I fell in love with them and they felt divine. "I'll take these," I declared.

"Excellent choice," they declared. Fiona continued, "Though I'd like to see Madam in higher heels someday, with ankle straps, I think."

"Perhaps the next time?" Darla suggested.

"Meanwhile," Fiona went on, "we must help Madam show her new shoes off."

"And show off her hose."

"And her lovely legs."

"Of course. Lovely legs and feet are what it's all about, after all."

"I don't understand," I said.

Darla winked at me. "Madam knows where legs lead to. Nice shoes draw attention to Madam's feet. From her feet, a lover's eyes are drawn up her legs. From there . . ."

"I don't have a lover," I interrupted.

"In those shoes and hose, Madam soon will," Darla assured me. "But it's all in how they are displayed. For example, if Madam would kindly cross her legs?"

I obeyed, left over right. Fiona plucked the shoe loose from my left heel and let it hang from my toes. "You see, Madam, how a dangling shoe draws the eyes? From the shoe, to the delicate elegance of Madam's foot, and then her ankle."

"And if Madam's skirt is arranged just so . . ." Darla adjusted the hem of my skirt across my thighs, just high enough to display a hint of the lacy tops of my stockings.

Both girls resumed their seats and took hold of my ankles once more.

Fiona said, "No sensuous man, or woman, could look at those feet, those legs, those stocking tops, and not be tempted to explore."

My left leg was lifted off my right. Both ankles were drawn forward, tilting me back into the leather depths of the bench seat. Fiona moved my left ankle up and farther left. Darla moved my right ankle up and to the right. My skirt fell back. Their eyes were directed up under my tumbling skirt. I should have felt embarrassed, and I was, but it was a curiously warm embarrassment that I found myself perfectly willing to endure.

My left ankle was planted on Fiona's right shoulder. Darla set my right on her left one. Once more, four hands stroked and kneaded my legs, working gradually higher, unhurriedly. Of the three of us, it seemed that only I felt any urgency. Thumbs worked my calves. Strong fingers manipulated my kneecaps. Two palms smoothed upward on each of my thighs. I tensed when I felt them glide over the lace at the tops of my stockings.

And then their hands were warm on my cool bare skin.

I held my breath. Surely they didn't mean to caress my thighs any higher. Fingertips traced little circles. Each circle took them higher, closer to my naked sex. I looked down at the girls through slitted eyelids. Their eyes were intent on what their fingers were doing, or perhaps were focused on my puckered slit, that I was sure was now exposed and leaking shamefully.

The girls knelt up on their stools and leaned in closer, tipping me onto my back with my legs V'ed high. A fingertip brushed the left lip of my pussy. Another stroked the right one. Very gently, I was teased open.

"Beautiful," Fiona sighed.

"Lovely," Darla agreed.

"Delicious aroma."

"Sweet, but with a hint of spice."

"After you."

"Why, thank you, Fiona."

Tender fingers spread me. I felt hot breath on my sex, and inside it. It'd been a while since I'd felt a tongue in there, but I recognized the sensation instantly. It lapped and probed and swirled and lapped again. I heard obscene sucking sounds. Darla's head worked from side to side, burrowing her face into me. She lifted, just a fraction, dragging the flat of her tongue upward between my lips. With a woman's sure instinct, she found the throbbing tip of my clitoris. Her tongue flicked on it. Her lips closed and sucked, drawing it out from its sheath. With it held secure, she trilled, vibrating my hard little pearl.

Darla lifted her head. Before my pussy had a chance to feel neglected, Fiona's mouth replaced the blonde's. Her tongue's tip made tight little circles. I became aware of fingers probing into me. One, or two, hooked up behind my pubic bone to find and massage my G-spot.

My eyelids slitted apart again. As the girls were now kneeling up on their stools, their skirts had fallen forward, to their narrow waists. Two heart-shaped bare bottoms were uppermost. Each girl had a hand moving behind her friend, no doubt fondling her intimately.

Somehow, they managed to spread my thighs so far apart that they could get both of their faces on my sex. I no longer knew whose tongue was squirming into me or whose was tantalizing my clit. At one point, it felt as if two tongues were inside me at once, kissing each other as they delved into my wetness.

Inevitably, I squealed and jerked as a delicious climax convulsed my insides.

The girls reared back, grinning, with my juices smeared across their young faces.

"That was, like, unreal," I told them.

"We're glad you liked it," Fiona said.

"You'll come again?" Darla asked me.

"Of course. Maybe next week?"

Fiona grinned. "No, Madam, you misunderstand. Of course we will be delighted to see you next week, but meanwhile, you'll come again."

They lifted my skirt back up and lowered their faces to my sex once more.

Hannah Irving

JennaTip #11: Foot and Shoe Fetish

Do you have a shoe fetish? Lots of women do. Not for men's tasseled loafers, but for chocolate brown, suede pumps with metal spike heels and cherry red stillettos that show off toe cleavage. Expensive, dangerous, sexy shoes that make the calves flex and the ass high(er) and tight(er). You probably don't need shoes to get off, but there are shoes out there that buying and owning is an orgasm in itself. But enough about the national shoe-buying obsession and on to what really is a foot or shoe fetish.

A fetish is really about sex and needing that object to actually get off. The dangling shoe, as the girls mention in the story, is really, truly one of the ways that shoe fetishists get off. It can also be a way that a woman gets off. Rocking your foot back and forth with your legs crossed can stimulate your clitoris. Some women reach orgasm.

Again with Chinese trivia: Chinese women had their feet bound for centuries because a Tang Dynasty emperor had a sexual fetish for women with small feet. He liked to be masturbated with their feet. It became a cultural phenomenon and small feet became thought of as sexually attractive because one man in power found them to be. It was also a status symbol because the women were crippled and unable to walk or work. It was only for the wealthy who could afford to have servants. The practice started around the tenth century and was finally outlawed in 1912.

This story is a sad comment on what has happened today to intimacy. We no longer talk to the person we are physically with but instead we are talking and texting some other person, and so are they. Why not go to dinner with the person you obviously would rather talk to than the person sitting across from you?

Hanging Up

Paul, my husband, was a very attentive lover. Once upon a time, not so very long ago, he would spend hours devoted to me, to my pleasure, to tasting me and touching me. Unfortunately, there might be no happily ever after to my story. That's still to be determined.

I had several lovers before Paul. None had been as attentive during and affectionate afterward when it came to our sex life. In fact, before we got married, just about a year ago, sex with Paul was an incredible, transcendent experience.

I cannot put an exact date on it, but sometime between the honeymoon and a few months later, sex became less of a thrill and occurred much less often. Paul seemed to have his cell phone glued to his ear, always talking to someone on the other end and no longer talking with me. It was getting in the way of our relationship, our friendship, and our sex life.

How had our sex become boring so quickly?

So, as a means of resurrecting our love life, I decided to take things into my own hands. I made arrangements to put the spark back through introducing some, um, items. I convinced him to come along with me so I could get his feedback, so to speak. That's how we ended up in front of Sally's Seduction, a

small boutique just outside the city limits in a secluded area surrounded by large evergreens.

We pulled into the parking lot and, as I gathered my things,
Paul ignored me in favor of his cell, per usual. As I was about to
get out of the car, however, a younger couple stepped out of the
shop. They were modestly attractive, rock-star thin and dressed
in ratty T-shirts and even rattier jeans. His bare arms were covered with detailed tattoos and both of them had enough face
piercings to cause them big problems with airport security.

On the way to their car, her walk became animated as she
swung a small shopping bag front and back. Almost like she was
teasing him with it. When he opened the front door, she slipped
a pair of handcuffs out of the bag and snapped one side onto her
wrist. They laughed and quickly he worked her arms behind her
and cuffed her other wrist.

"What the hell are they doing?" Paul had at last noticed something, but his lips were still pressed to his phone. "No, no. I
wasn't talking to you," he had to explain.

Then Paul did an unusual thing—for him. He said, "Hold
on," and pulled the phone away from his face.

Not caring if they had an audience, the guy slid his hand
under her shirt as she playfully wiggled her shoulders and lightly
kicked at his shins. Soon, he had her shirt above her breasts and
was stroking them. He kissed one, then the other. Then, like a
dancer, he spun her around so she faced into the car.

"I'll call you back," Paul said, then flipped the phone closed.
He sat there, next to me, silently watching. For the first time in
what seemed like forever, Paul's undivided attention was focused
on something besides his phone. It wasn't me, but it was an improvement. After catching a slight smile on his lips, I dropped a
hand to his lap and felt his hard-on pressing firmly against the
seam of his pants.

With one hand, the guy kept grabbing at his girlfriend's tits from behind as he used the other hand to tug down her jeans. Once the pants had fallen to her ankles, he pushed her into the front seat, facedown. His pants dropped next and the last thing my husband and I saw before the car door closed was his skinny, white ass on top of her.

Paul's visceral reaction to the scene made me even more eager to get inside the store.

Once inside, we walked around the shop and browsed for a bit. Well, I browsed and Paul talked on his cell phone again. That damn phone. Nothing really caught my eye. It was the typical sex shop. There was an array of stripper shoes by the wall, cheaply packaged dildos by the dozen, and a large display of novelty condoms and lubricants. A few trashy outfits lined with feather boas were hanging limply from a rack. Nothing really my style.

As I walked toward the wall of vibrators and jelly cocks, I noticed a side doorway covered by a heavy, velvety black curtain. Another room?

Sally's sultry voice answered my unspoken question. "It's my other store. For the less-mainstream clientele." Her juicy red lips went up in a smirk. I hadn't seen her before. She must have been bent down behind the counter.

Sally was a few years older than me, blond, short, and a little overweight—but she still looked great in her corset, miniskirt, and thigh-high boots. I could tell that Paul was equally impressed because he suddenly lost focus on his phone call, stuttering an apology and asking the person on the other end to repeat basically everything.

Leading Paul toward the room, I pushed past the curtain. Now this was more like it. Sexy bustiers made of black leather or latex. Corsets lined with leather and silver buckles. Stiletto boots made of black leather.

Paul seemed impressed. He didn't turn off the phone, but he definitely eyed some of the panty-and-bra sets. While he still listened, he was talking less and less, just grunts of acknowledgment. I picked up a sheer black net lace bra. It had leather straps, cut wide and criss-crossing in front and around the see-through cups. The lace was slit at the nipple area and I bet my brown nipples would poke through the slit nicely. I had to try it on.

I held a leather micro-mini to my waist. "Red or black?"

Paul nudged me as he walked by. He mouthed the word, "Black."

I picked the black skirt.

Shoes. I'm a sucker for high heels. The black boots with platforms were much too chunky. A pair of simple black heels caught my eye. Four-inch heels. Straps around the ankle. Like sexed-up Mary Janes. I picked those.

Paul was still talking shop. I needed something spicier. I noticed a box filled with strips of fabric. Assorted silk scarves. They'd be perfect. I took four from the pile.

"What are those for?" Paul asked.

I showed him my wrists and his dark eyes gleamed. Handing him the goodies, I led him out of the room.

Sally was by the counter. "You need a dressing room?"

I nodded. I couldn't wait to try on the bra. I couldn't wait to try it all on, and the shoes, God, I almost came just looking at them.

As she unlocked a room, she spoke in that sexy voice. "You're my last customers for the day." Her gaze dropped to my breasts. "If you need anything, holler."

It was a typical dressing room, maybe a bit bigger. Full-length mirrors covered three sides with a long bench in black velvet next to the center of the three. I put the clothes and accessories on the bench. Paul sat on a chair next to it and stretched out his long legs. Then he picked up the phone again.

I turned around and dropped my shorts. I stepped into the skirt and slid it over my thighs, pulling the fabric over my hips. It was tight, but I managed to zip up the side. The soft leather clung to my curves. I always wanted more back, and the skirt worked what I had.

Still holding the phone to his ear, Paul smacked me on the ass and gave me a thumbs-up. Then he went back to his call. To keep his attention, I needed to pull out the big guns.

I pulled my shirt over my head. Unhooked my bra and tossed it at him. The strap caught on his ear and hung down like an ornament. Then I turned my back to him and tried on the net bra, my brown nipples peeking through the holes just as I imagined. With my hands on my hips, I turned and faced Paul.

He stopped mid-call and snapped his phone shut. Finally! I had his attention. He watched me slip on the heels. Propping my foot on the bench, I fastened first one strap around my ankle, then the other strap around the other ankle.

"How do I look?" I asked.

"Delicious." He picked up one of the scarves. "And what do we do with these?"

"Well, that's really up to you," I winked.

"Oh, really?"

"Have your way with me." I smiled.

I stepped closer to the bench, my breasts swaying in their encasements, easily within kissing distance of his mouth. He grabbed my waist and pulled me closer.

Paul's mouth burrowed between my breasts, taking one nipple into his mouth and then the other. Back and forth he went until I was sloppy wet. His hand peeled my skirt up, exposing my ass. His hand smacked me lightly, and I giggled.

"I like that."

"Oh, do you? Such a naughty girl." Paul was definitely getting into it.

"That's right." I admitted.

"With a spankable ass." He smacked me harder this time.

I glanced over my shoulder and hoped that Sally couldn't hear those spanks. Then Paul slapped my ass again, gaining my full attention.

"Hands behind your back," Paul insisted and I complied. He used a scarf to tie my wrists together. I stared at my reflection. Hands tied and helpless. Hard nipples poking through the bra. Bare bottom exposed and marked with pink handprints. I had a wild look in my eyes. I almost didn't recognize myself.

And then it happened. Again. Paul's cell phone vibrated and chimed.

My breath held as Paul's eyes jumped from me, to the phone, and back again. Damn. I knew it. He was going to pick the call over me. Leave me stuck there with my hands tied, my breath panting.

Paul took the phone, opened the dressing room door, and tossed it down the hall. Soon he was whispering into my ear. "Where were we?"

I finally had my husband back. And it looked like all it was going to take was a trip to Sally's Seduction to get him off his cell and back to getting me off instead. What a pleasant reward for my taking such initiative.

Between the parking lot scene and my fashion show, I had his full attention.

I kept on hoping that Sally, the shop owner, didn't hear all the noise.

Paul chuckled and looked me up and down. He pulled the micro-mini skirt up even farther and he smacked me even harder. Then his fingertips touched me and he whispered, "So very wet. Shame on you. What should I do with such a naughty girl?"

"With such a spankable ass," I added and then watched him unbuckle his belt. I was going to find out.

I was completely exposed—my hands bound and my skirt hiked all the way up. I wanted to touch myself, to feel how wet this made me. Soon I didn't need to touch to tell because the wetness pooled between my legs and I could feel it dripping from my lips to my thighs.

Paul put his fingers between my legs, sending shivers throughout my body. I grinned as he caressed my clit. Was he going to fuck me right here? Would he spank me afterward?

He grabbed me by the waist. Pulled my face down over his lap. He rubbed my ass with one hand, held me down with the other.

Without another word, he smacked my right butt cheek. Then the left. Back and forth. The sound of his hand slapping my ass sounded loud. I glanced toward the door.

"Worried about our friend?" I saw Paul's grin in the mirror.

"What if she hears us?"

"I'm sure she does. She hasn't kicked us out by now. I bet she's by the door. Waiting. Wondering when I'll fuck you."

If she opened the door, she'd see my pink ass. The thought filled me with shame. And excitement. We'd never played in public before. The image aroused me even more.

Paul slid his fingers between my thighs. "You would like that, wouldn't you?"

I moaned.

"I bet she's right by the door. Waiting for an invitation." He helped me off his lap.

"What are you doing?" I felt him untie the scarf.

He spun me around. Bent me forward to place my hands on the bench. With the heels, I was the perfect height for him. I heard him unzip. Watched his face as he slid into me.

"God, you're so wet." He thrust into me hard. "So fucking wet."

I tried to keep quiet. Tried to keep the moans inside. I gave up. It was too much. Seeing his eyes glow as he fucked me. The way my breasts bounced with every thrust. Watching myself get a hard fuck. The glazed look in my eyes, my slightly parted lips.

He fucked me harder. I couldn't stop moaning. I completely forgot where we were. It didn't matter. I concentrated on his hard cock, on the way his hands felt on my hips. Just inches away from my pink ass.

As if reading my mind, he slapped my ass. Again and again. Keeping with the rhythm of his thrusts. We moaned and grunted like animals.

Until we heard a soft knock on the door.

Paul paused in mid-action. Still inside me, he said, "Yes?" Always the calm one. His hands kept me in place with my legs still spread.

We heard Sally's amused voice. "You two okay in there?"

Paul squeezed my butt cheeks. Hard enough to make me squirm. He wanted me to answer.

"We're fine," I said. Fine? What was I thinking? It was the first word that popped into my head.

"Did one of you lose a phone? I found one in the hall. Can't get the thing to stop vibrating." Her throaty laugh was close, like she had her lips right next to the door.

That damn phone. I swear, it was like a bad penny. We couldn't throw it away without it turning up every time we turned around.

Paul pulled out. He glanced at the door, then glanced at me.

I knew what he was thinking. I'd been thinking the same thing. Did I dare?

He wouldn't pressure me to do anything I didn't want to do. I put my hand on the door while he smiled and sat back on the bench.

I pushed open the door. Sally's red lips were wet, ripe, ready to be kissed. When I stepped forward, she grinned and said, "It looks like you're busy."

Paul's calm voice, "Not at all. In fact, we could use a little help here."

I couldn't believe my husband. I wouldn't have been so bold, but it turns out that Sally was just as bold. Without another word, she stepped forward, cupped my left breast, and stuck her tongue in my mouth. She bent her head, moving her hot mouth over my nipples.

Paul's hands backed me toward him. Sally followed. I sat on his lap, still facing her. Rubbed against Paul's hard-on while Sally took off her top to expose her gorgeous breasts. The nipples were pale and flat and so big.

I touched them. It was the first time I had seen another woman up close. I massaged her breasts, and she moaned. But Paul quickly pulled my hands back and used a silk scarf to tie them up again.

"Isn't this how we're doing it today?" he asked without expecting an answer. I wasn't being given any options.

I struggled a little and pouted.

I'd never been sexually attracted to women before, at least not like this. But that moment, in that small, dressing room, with my husband and me exposed and Sally topless, I had the urge to go wild on her. And because of Paul and the silk scarves that bound me, the most I could do was sit.

But Sally was okay with . . . with whatever. I saw Paul watching our reflection. With three mirrors, he could see us from most angles. If he wanted a show, he'd be able to experience it in 3-D.

While Paul held me in place with his arms around my waist, Sally moved in. Her long, white fingernails toyed with my nipples, then with my breasts. She soon lowered her lips to my breasts and removed her hands and placed her palm flat against my mons.

Paul suddenly took a quick, deep breath and I figured her fingertips were caressing his cock as the palm of her hand pressed against me.

I lifted up onto my feet, knees bent, my situation very precarious, but I had to give her better access. Then, feeling so aroused at my absolutely craven behavior, I felt my muscles tightening. I was on the verge of coming just thinking about—and, of course, viewing in the mirrors—what Paul and I were doing.

Paul had tied the knot around my wrists so tight that I really didn't think I could break it. And his grip on my waist was just as tight. I wanted to touch Sally in every way she was touching me. I wanted to get fucked by, and fuck, both of them. But I was constantly reminded that I was just their toy. And that thought aroused me even more.

Soon, Sally was on her knees in front of me, teasing me with her tongue, nipping at me with her lips. Then she stopped and a moment later, Paul sighed. I could only imagine that her lips had moved from my clit to Paul's cock and balls. I tried to see in the mirror but my view was blocked by Paul's back and my own thighs.

She alternated between us a few times. Then, using her hands, she guided Paul's hard-on into me. Sally kept on her knees, licking me, licking him. Watching Paul thrust into me while my hips bounced. Sally kept her mouth close to our bodies until he came in me and I came on him.

We three collapsed in slow motion to the floor. Four breasts heaving. One of my legs across Sally's shoulder while she rested her head on my other thigh. Paul's arms were still wrapped around my waist. His lips pressed against my neck.

We would have made a great museum statue.

"Would someone please untie me?" I finally asked.

I bought every piece of clothing that I'd picked out. Sally even gave us a huge discount on it all. Not because of the sex. That would have been tacky.

But because all of it was used.

Stacey Newman

This story is short. It doesn't have a lot of blatant sex. It is just so perfect and funny. In the end, I hope it knocks your socks off . . . but not the shoes!

Four Queens

The poker tournament was only a week away, so four of us decided to get together for some practice. In his midthirties, Doc was the oldest. He wasn't a real doctor. He just had a way of staring at everyone's cards as though he could diagnose how good they were. Then there was Burger, a skinny guy who liked fast food so much that we always had to warn him not to get secret sauces all over the cards. Max was the only guy without a nickname. Attractive, neatly dressed, he didn't say much. Not usually. Except for when he won, he'd almost uncontrollably shout, "Yes!"

Me? They called me Cherry after the color of the stiletto heels I always wore when playing poker. My good-luck charms. And who cared if they looked weird with blue jeans and a sweatshirt top? A charm is a charm.

We'd all gotten together a few times before. They were a good group. Even though I was the only woman, they never let on that they noticed. We were all just into playing cards—and each other. Or so I once thought.

That night my good-luck charms were working overtime. I kicked their asses most of the night and had a mountain of chips to prove it. Burger still had enough cash for a few fried-fish sandwiches. But the other guys were close to broke. Doc was the genius who suggested strip poker and I was the first fool to agree. Hell, I'd been winning all night and I still felt a lot of luck left in those tall heels of mine.

But it wasn't long after we switched from money to clothes

that I needed that pile of chips to hide my lacy pink bra. Doc, down to his boxers, was doing even worse. But Burger and Max still owned most of their clothes and were gawking at me like I was a cold beer on a sunny Superbowl Sunday afternoon.

I tapped my heels against the table leg as I drew my latest hand. It was good. Really good. And I felt my blush being replaced by pride.

"How about all or nothing, fools? Fold and keep your clothes. Or stay in and losers strip all the way down." I kept my words cold, my stare icy. I'm sure they couldn't tell if I was bluffing or if I had killer cards.

Doc's and Burger's cards dropped faster than a slot machine coin. But Max quietly matched my stare and called me.

I was so confident that my ladies would save me that, after I'd thrown down four queens, I bounced up, hands on hips, ready to do a victory dance.

"Not so fast, Cherry," Max said as he covered my queens with a straight flush.

Damn. How did the night go from me raking in the chips to me standing there wearing just panties and a bra in a room full of guys, and owing? Like most gamblers at some time during their careers, I wished I could have taken back the last hour.

But it wasn't going to happen.

Doc was the one who started chanting, "Bra . . . bra . . . bra . . ." Soon Burger and Max joined in, making an offbeat chorus.

I flipped them double birds, just to shut them up a little, then began strutting around the table. Not so that they'd get a better show. More just to stall for some time.

But they continued their chant, "Bra . . . bra . . . bra . . ." as the stiletto heels forced my calves to tighten, causing my legs to look longer and firmer. Then, after a quick chug of air, I yanked off the bra and flashed the boys two more queens.

"Yes!" Max cheered.

"Damn, girl, why haven't I noticed those before?" cried Burger.

Doc just started chanting a different tune. "Panties . . . panties . . . panties . . ." And, as before, the others chimed in.

I started cruising around on those stilettos again, feeling their eyes following each step. Finally I figured it was probably best to just get it over with. With barely a thought, I wrestled my panties down and off, then stood there, breasts heaving, in as defiant a pose as I could imagine.

Suddenly the boys were so quiet that you could have heard the king of hearts wink. Probably because they hadn't imagined me as the shaved type. Bathed in that silence, I swung a foot onto a chair seat and began to undo the strap of one of my red stilettos.

Max was the one to begin the next chorus and the others quickly joined in.

"Not the shoes . . . not the shoes . . . not the shoes . . ."

Oscar West

I wasn't sure about the ending on this one, but so much of it is so wonderfully funny and sexy, I had to include it.

Three Steps

"They were eyeing you," my boyfriend said of the bouncers by the strip joint's entrance.

"They eye everyone, Frank. It's their job to eye people." Frank was the most jealous person I'd ever known. He was wonderful in all other ways, loving and kind, giving, attentive, but so suspicious of other men that it drove me crazy.

We'd been dating for almost three years and the more serious the relationship got, the more possessive he became. At first it was hardly noticeable. Then as we got more involved, it progressed. I did everything I could to change things. I rarely wore provocative clothing—just simple shirts and slacks. I didn't talk to random men in bars or parties. I constantly assured Frank that I loved him and would never disappoint him.

But things just kept getting worse. When it finally was unbearable, it was too late for me to just end it cleanly. We lived together. We had a joint account. And I did love him.

It wasn't just that he was jealous. His behavior at times was downright bizarre. For example, he saw no problem taking me to a strip club where he could ogle other women naked but was upset when the bouncers checked out my ID. Is that a double standard, or what?

When we first started dating, I anticipated challenges, but nothing like this. Frank is tall enough to blend into a basketball team and I stand a few inches shy of five feet. He is business-stylish. I feel best in blue jeans and a T-shirt. Oh, and the color thing. Frank is whiter than George Clooney's smile and I'm as black as Tiger's wood.

I steered us over to a small table near the stage, knowing he'd want to be up close and personal with the talent, and we sat down on a pair of wooden chairs with high backs. They looked out of place in this strip club, more like they should be in my mother's kitchen, but Frank didn't notice. He never notices anything other than the naked girls and if another man so much as glances my way. Frank would be at it again, even before the waitress asked us for our drink order.

"The guys in here are staring at you." His eyes were narrow, swiveling slowly from side to side.

"Gee, Frank. You think? It's a strip club. Aren't guys supposed to stare at women in here?"

"Drinks?" Our waitress ended the debate. She was, as expected, attractive and dressed in an outfit so skimpy and tight that I could count her ribs. Our margaritas came at the same moment that the first dancer stepped onto the stage.

She was tall and leggy, dressed in a white bridal corset, her reddish blond hair up in a bun. Her looks were as stunning as her dancing was bad. Her feet couldn't keep a beat. She stumbled when she should have slid. She was as awkward as a one-legged skateboarder on a staircase.

Not one of the men in that place seemed to care, and they cared less and less as she showed more and more of her skin.

Frank became a cheerleader. He bounced around his chair, alternately clapping his palms and rocking his fists, while he shouted and hooted louder than anyone else.

I sat there, my legs tight together and hands on my lap. Frank would be horrified if he knew, but all I could think about was how much better I could dance on that stage.

Not soon enough, she was done. As another stripper began her show, the first started walking around the audience looking for drink offers and lap dance tips.

"Wasn't she great!" Frank was shaking with enthusiasm.

"Frank." I had a problem. Frank cocked his head in my direction but kept his eyes on the stage.

"Listen. Don't you think it's weird that you're so jealous over me, but it's okay for you to hoot at other women? Naked women?"

He looked at me like I was crazy.

The conversation ended when the first stripper came to our table and smiled at both of us. "My name's Christy. Having fun?"

Frank started rooting and clapping like she was his favorite football team. She laughed and smiled, fake as a politician.

"Want a lap dance, honey?" she asked Frank, then turned to me. "If that's all right with you."

I shrugged my shoulders. Frank nodded like his neck was on a spring.

"Twenty dollars," she suggested. Frank's fingers fumbled through his pockets. His look told me he was cash broke.

"You want me to pay?" I couldn't believe this. I grabbed my purse and paid.

Christy didn't hesitate once she'd tucked the bill into her cleavage. From somewhere, she produced a pair of gold handcuffs.

"Now put your arms behind you, through the chair back." Christy said it as though this was a part of a doctor's physical. And Frank did it.

As Christy cuffed Frank's wrists behind his back and through the chair, she explained that while she could touch the customers, it was illegal for the customers to touch her. The handcuffs were a simple way for Frank to obey the law. First she acted like she was going to start the lap dance by circling Frank but then, with her hands on his shoulders from behind, she leaned down to his ear and whispered, "Frank, I'm Dr. Marks. Your girlfriend, Lori, has engaged my services to help break you of your incredibly unhealthy jealousy."

Frank tried to stand. He arched his back, straining against the cuffs, but couldn't break free. Dr. Marks pressed down with her hands on his shoulders and he finally stopped struggling.

"Frank. You need to stay calm. Lori loves you. Only you. But your relationship will die if you continue down the road you're traveling. Do you understand what I am saying to you?"

Frank glared at her over his shoulder but then nodded.

She told him that tonight was a do-or-die intervention that either worked, or it didn't. If it did, then he would be cured and our relationship would be back on track. If it didn't, then I would leave that night and never see him again.

He was shocked, angry, frustrated—and, I think, really scared.

"Frank. Lori is going to step up to the stage now."

His eyes bugged out and he started to protest but Dr. Marks placed a finger over his lips, and told him that his objection would count against him and that he'd be better off simply allowing the events to unfold.

So, with Frank cuffed in place and forced to face the stage, I climbed the stairs and stood in the middle, with one hand grasping the brassy pole and the other on my hip.

Frank didn't know, but on top of being a former cheerleader and dancer, I had also taken some stripping classes once upon a time and knew my way around a pole and stage, although I had never once actually stripped.

I took a deep breath, nodded my head twice, and the music started.

Of course, the guys in the club, because this was a real strip club, all started yelling for me to take something off. Anything off.

Frank tried so hard to stand up to grab me off the stage, he knocked Dr. Marks right over, but he wasn't getting loose. Dr. Marks gave him a warning wag of her finger, grabbed his jaw in her hand, and twisted his head back to the stage to watch me.

I continued dancing, finally pulling my shirt up so my belly was exposed. I'm not a hard body anymore, but I'm juicy and sexy and I love my curves. Anyway, this was for me and I didn't really give a shit if the guys thought I was hot or not. I knew I was hot.

After a bit longer, I undid my belt, buttons, and fly. I wiggled and even jiggled a little.

I started really getting into it. The crowd reacted with begs and cheers.

So I gave it to them. Staring Frank in the eyes, I whipped off my shirt and bra. My breasts leapt out, nipples hard. The crowd howled.

By the time I hopped off that stage I was down to just panties and socks.

Frank looked relieved that I was off the stage and out of the spotlight, but if he didn't pass the test, then there was going to be more. I was ready for it. I knew this was the only way and I was willing to do everything I could to save us.

"Frank." Dr. Marks spoke to him slowly, getting his eyes away from me walking mostly nude through the crowd. "What did you think of Lori's performance?"

At first, Frank couldn't seem to form words, like his mouth was stuffed with cotton. He swallowed several times and said, loudly and clearly, "Lori acted like a whore. If she gets dressed immediately and we go home and she promises to never, ever, ever do anything like that again, I will consider forgiving her."

"Wrong answer, Frank!" Dr. Marks shook her head and made tsking sounds with her tongue and teeth.

"I'm sorry, Lori. Frank did not respond well to Step 1—"

"What the hell do you mean, Step 1?" Frank snarled.

Dr. Marks put another finger to his lips and continued as though he hadn't interrupted. "So you need to take this to Step 2 or decide to walk away now forever."

I looked at Frank. I looked in his eyes and saw real fear. Sure, he was upset and angry, but I think he was terrified that I would walk.

"Frank, honey, do you want to see if Step 2 will help? Are you willing to honestly try to end this jealousy, or should I just go?" I asked, softly.

He was obviously conflicted but finally he lowered his head in defeat and whispered, "Let's try Step 2."

Time to ramp it up.

I walked over to the nearest guy. He sat tall in his chair, near enough to Frank that he could hear and see me. Dark hair, dressed metro with a sloppy tie and striped shirt.

"You want a lap dance?" I asked him.

Wide-eyed, he nodded yes.

"I have to charge you. How about a dollar?"

The guy dug in his pockets and came up with three quarters, two dimes, and a nickel. I took the change and tossed it on the stage.

"I have to tie your hands behind your back. It's the law," I explained as I peeled off my panties and reached behind him. I tied his hands behind his back, my nipples rubbing against his stomach as I worked. Then I sprang up to the tops of my toes, looked over at Frank, and said, "I'm doing this for you because I love you."

The guy I was about to dance for looked behind him, totally confused, but I didn't give him a chance to back out.

Frank struggled against the cuffs and chair as I turned away from my customer and bent over and pointed my ass upward, grinding against the air. But a warning look from Dr. Marks settled him down pretty quickly. Frank was still grinding his teeth, though. I could hear them.

I couldn't see if my customer liked it or not, but the rest of the crowd did. Guys and gals started to clap and shout.

I decided it would be better to look at the customer. I would also be able to look over his shoulder to watch Frank. So I turned around. Wrinkling his hair with my fingers, I bounced my chest around, up and down, and to the sides while my hips made circles. All the time I kept my eyes on Frank's.

I wasn't sure how much my customer was enjoying this. There was a rise in his pants, but it wasn't too impressive. He kept looking down.

I pressed my cleavage against his mouth. He stuck his tongue out and licked. But as soon as I backed off, he was looking down again.

I finally figured out what he was looking at. My socks. The only clothes I had on.

I smiled at Frank. When he realized I was going to remove my socks, Frank started bouncing the chair toward me, like those little bits of cotton were my last shield. He didn't get anywhere, but fell on the floor to the side.

Ouch. That must have hurt.

I slipped off my socks and moved a bare foot onto my patron's lap. He liked that. A lot. His eyes flashed on like a lightbulb. So I pulled up my own chair, sat down, and planted both feet in his seat. I rubbed his lap with my heel as my toes danced across his stomach. My purple-painted toenails glistened in the dim lighting.

Somehow, the guy's fly got unzipped and spread enough so that his cock snuck out. Okay, I cheated, I did it by leaning in with my fingers. Then my toes used his precome to juice up his shaft. The ball of my foot began to stroke him as his lips grew wet. I took a break to stand up and peek over his shoulder at Frank again. Then I was back to rubbing that guy's cock with all my sole until he moaned and shook uncontrollably. His come speckled my purple toenails and soaked in between my toes.

I looked over at Frank again. He was nearly purple himself, spitting mad and rocking back and forth. A bouncer came up with Dr. Marks and lifted him, chair and all, and placed him back upright.

"Frank. Please control yourself," Dr. Marks said reprovingly. "You're making a scene. A completely unnecessary scene, I might add."

"Get these damn cuffs off me right now, you bitch." Frank even spit at her.

"Frank. I think that you have failed Step 2. Just so you realize, there are only three steps. You have one more opportunity, if Lori is willing to grant it, so I'd decide right now just how much you love Lori and whether you get control."

It amazed me how calm and serene she was in the face of his anger, but it worked. He took several gulping breaths, swallowed hard, and then tried to speak. He had to stop and start several times before he got the words out without expletives.

"I love Lori. I am ready for Step 3. Nothing you do can be worse than Step 2. Nothing." He said this last part in a small voice, as though afraid to tempt us to prove him wrong.

Stage 3. Was I ready? Yes. Yes, I was. I promised going into this that I would take it all the way if need be. Well, the need was there. I was up to the challenge. All for love.

Dr. Marks motioned with her finger to a man standing over to the side to join us. He walked over. He was tall, not as tall as Frank, but still a good six feet something. He was very attractive. Wavy dark hair, green eyes, and a bit of dark stubble sprinkling his jaw. He was breathtaking, actually.

Frank saw him coming over and spittle started to form in the corners of his mouth. I feared a new onslaught of screaming, but one look at Dr. Marks and he calmed right down.

Dr. Marks introduced the man simply as Mick. He smiled and took my hand in his, leaning in to kiss me on the cheek. "Hello."

I thought Frank would burst a vein, they bulged out of his neck so prominently, but again, he managed to regain control.

Mick said hello to Frank and then kissed Dr. Marks, too. Then he took her hand and my hand and led us over to a set of more comfortable chairs, against the wall. When we had had our exploratory session and Dr. Marks heard about my problems with Frank, she outlined her different programs. Step 3 was the most intense, but it had the greatest success rate without backsliding.

For this third part, Dr. Marks had explained to me that Mick was like a catalyst, and that she and I were basically inert material left to our own devices. When Mick was added to the mix, however, we would become highly combustible. I majored in communications, not chemistry, so I wasn't so clear about what she meant, but I figured it was a metaphor and I'd understand soon enough.

I did.

I'm not bisexual. I'm not bi-curious. I have never fantasized about kissing another woman, or touching her, or being touched by her, but suddenly, with Mick as the instigator, Dr. Marks and I were caressing one another, each on a separate side of Mick. He had one hand around each of us, gripping our waists and then our hips. He spread his legs apart, pushing his thighs against my stomach as I was turned almost fully to the side to have better access to Dr. Marks. I was still totally nude and Dr. Marks hadn't dressed again after her strip charade, so there was plenty of soft, silky skin available.

Mick moved his hands down and over from my hip to my exposed ass. He curved his hand around with his fingers delving between my legs.

I was surprised but pleasantly so, and so wet and turned on, he was drenched in moments. I learned that Dr. Marks was as well when he brought his hands away from us and then crossed his hands in front of him and had us each lick the other's slickness off his fingers.

I almost forgot about Frank. Almost. I looked over at him. He sat, cuffed and slack-jawed, watching the show. He wasn't struggling. He wasn't screaming or cussing. He was simply staring at me like he'd never seen me before, and he hadn't. Not this me.

I mouthed, "I love you. Only you."

He blinked. He licked his lips and looked pale, but then he smiled. At first it was tentative, but it grew stronger and brighter, until it lit up his face and he yelled, "I love you, too. Lori, I love you."

I pulled away from Mick and Dr. Marks. They'd both continued touching and caressing me while I looked over at Frank, but I hadn't even felt it.

Frank realized this. He saw then that other people wanting me, looking at me, talking to me, even touching me couldn't touch us. Could not erase our love.

I asked Dr. Marks for the key to the cuffs. She pulled it off a thin chain she wore around her neck and smiled at me, then went back to Mick.

I walked across the room full of people, but it was as though we were completely alone. I only had eyes for Frank and he finally knew it.

After I set him free, he stood, towering over me, then leaned down, down, down to put his head at my level. He put his arms around me, embracing me and lifting me up in the air. He kissed me gently, then leaned in and whispered, "Where'd you learn to do that with your feet?"

Corinne Uecker

JennaTip #12: Dealing with Jealousy

A little bit of jealousy is not uncommon and really isn't unhealthy. There's a great old tune about how he gets jealous because he knows she likes him to be a little jealous, as it reinforces for her that she is important to him. A little jealousy can make you feel that way, but too much jealousy, the kind where you have to change how you dress or who you talk to or the kind that leaves you always worried about him or her getting angry—that kind is dangerous.

Strong women can end up in relationships that aren't healthy. Highly educated women can as well. It isn't something that happens to just a certain kind of woman (or man). It is, unfortunately, a widespread problem when jealousy and violence meet. If you are in a dangerous relationship, you do not have to accept it. No matter what you have been told. No matter if you think that you've said or done something wrong. No one, and that means *no one*, has the right to hit you, intimidate you, threaten you, or keep you emotionally or physically hostage.

Get some help. Be strong and get away.

There are many local, regional, and national organizations devoted to helping survivors of abuse. Call your local police station and ask for information and help. Please. Be safe.

Living a great life is the best revenge, but I think this story comes in a close second.

The Prick, the Dick, and the Chick

I had everything I needed for the night. I went through my mental checklist.

Sexy outfit. *Check.* New hair and makeup. *Check.* A fresh bottle of liquid courage. *Check.* A bag full of goodies from the local adult store. *Check and double-check.* I was set.

I kept hearing my ex-boyfriend Matt's voice in my head: "Sorry, but you're boring . . . in bed. I'm just not interested. You're too vanilla. If that ever changes, give me a call."

What a tool.

For a moment, I hated him. But then I figured he was probably right. I'd been brought up a good Catholic girl: kneesocks, plaid skirts, a ton of repressed sexual feelings. I thought I'd broken out of the guilt, but even though I like sex—I really do—I never have been able to relax, step outside myself, and just let go and do what I want, when I want, the exact way I want.

I needed a new me. A more exciting me.

It was going to take more than dyeing my hair and buying some sexier clothes, though that's where I started. So, here I was, hair auburn, clothes tighter and shorter, ready to try out the newer, more exciting me.

As said, I didn't only dye my hair and buy some new clothes. I bought a few other goodies. The accessories I checked and double-checked on my list.

One of them terrified and titillated me each time I so much as thought about it. It was leather and shiny buckles, with a hole. It criss-crossed my body, and *the hole* was right between my legs. But this hole wasn't meant to allow access to my own warm pink hole. It was for Carlos. Carlos being the name I'd given to my beautiful, decadent cock. I felt anything but vanilla as I prepared to undergo my own awakening.

Picking Carlos had required a separate shopping trip devoted entirely to his acquisition.

At the adult store, I snuck across the parking lot furtively looking over my shoulder with every third step, expecting to find my mother or one of her friends staring back intently at me, taking notes in a small book. As if! I even imagined them jumping out at me from behind the Dumpster in the corner of the lot. It reminded me of how I felt each time I was out at a party and not at the movies like I'd told them when I was in high school. I just knew they were going to suddenly appear and I'd be grounded. Silly, I know, but adult though I'd become it seemed that at times I was only an adult because I'd had more birthdays and not ever actually grown up.

I think, in a way, that's part of what was behind everything I was about to do. I was finally ready to grow up and be me and not pretend to be the girl my mom wanted me to be.

Sure, there was a lot of that girl still in me, but there was a wicked, sexy, naughty me deep inside and it was time for her to come out and play.

I took a deep breath, pushed open the door, and began searching in earnest. I found one lovely, artistic replica of a nice solid cock made of black glass with a row of gems around the base that I was sorely tempted to buy. It was so sleek and curvy that it could be used as a prop in a science fiction flick. I was a little worried about wearing it, though I did think it would have looked wonderful as the centerpiece on my dining table—just not for dinner with my grandparents.

Then I spotted another that I would have had to be blind to miss. It was pink. I liked that. Not Caucasian pink, but hot, bright pink. But it wasn't very long and would stick out . . . stand out . . . whatever . . . too much.

Finally I found one that was different from the rest. It was more realistic, the stem having a slightly pinkish hue. Simulated veins ran the length of its pronounced arc, giving it some real texture.

Perfect. I bought two and came home to get ready. I was preparing for the party of the year, the one for the wild and definitely anti-vanilla set. The party where I intended to shed my good-girl exterior and release my inner porn star, or something like that.

I squeezed into my black skinny jeans. I'd been dieting for a week to fit into them. I then slid the harness over my legs and crotch. Two straps criss-crossed my ass, and twin gold buckles attached on the side, which placed the triangular, leather flap on my front. In the flap was the circular hole with button snaps. The dildo would fit through that hole with the base kept in place by the leather. With the straps tight and the buttons snapped, the faux cock stood out like a man with a massive erection.

I chose a simple top. Just a sheer white blouse, nothing underneath. The white accentuated my dark nipples, making my small breasts appear fuller. The black leather straps crossing my torso looked pretty cool, too. I contemplated putting black pasties over my nipples. The other clubbers would be wearing much less. I decided the blouse was enough and the pasties too much.

A short time later, I rolled into the driveway of a house. No, not a house. It looked more like a museum. The driveway, longer than some toll roads, was lined with statues. The stone arch over the front entrance, sided by a dozen marble columns, looked as inviting as the Bastille.

And this was where the party was. The annual Gender Bender Ball. It was the biggest Halloween party on the West Coast. It brought people from all over the country. For one night you could be anyone or do anything or do anyone and be anything. It was a perfect start to finding the new, adult me. And by adult, I think I really do mean triple X.

I sat there for some time. Lights on, windows up. It would have been so easy to just turn around and go home. A deep breath. Then three more, and I was out of the car.

The line was short, and soon I was surrounded by countless sweating, dancing bodies. The entire downstairs seemed to be one big room surrounding a curving staircase. The DJ was spinning the latest house music, and the stage was covered with tall, lithe go-go dancers: men in tight shorts and women wearing nothing but body paint and white boots.

My outfit, the one that I thought was so daring, was more on the plain side. I'd never seen so many half-nude bodies in one place. Actually I'd have to say I'd never seen so many half-nude bodies in my lifetime, and remember, I went to an all-girl Catholic school for my entire education, sharing locker rooms and showers with lots of nude girls. Those girls did nothing to prepare me for what I was seeing tonight. Most of the women wore some sort of lingerie, but many chose the topless look. In my sheer top, I felt overdressed.

A lot of the men were even more outrageous. I saw one wearing nothing but matching nipple rings with a chain leading down to a spiked cock ring that circled his engorged, purple penis. There were plenty of drag queens in all shapes and sizes. Some of the men were prettier than I was. Damn their tight butts and flat tummies. With the flashing lights and thumping music, gender and sexual orientation became meaningless. Men kissing men, women grinding women, and couples touching other partners. It was a stand-up orgy of tits and cocks—a hedonistic romp set among a bedroom community.

It was the one event of the year that Matt always attended. Every year he wanted me to go, but I always told him the same thing. Not my style. Not my thing. He teased that I was too boring. At least I always thought it was just teasing, but now I guess he was just being honest about what he thought about me.

We'd see who was right. When he saw my outfit, he'd have a heart attack. First, I had to find him. It was going to be harder than I thought. There were too many bodies, too much motion, too much of too much.

I slinked past the main crowd, toward the bar area. Often, my dildo bumped into a gyrating body. No one ever minded. One man paused to wink and shake it in his hand.

I finally made it to the main bar. Still no Matt. I figured he'd show up here sooner or later.

A petite woman stepped up to me and smiled. A black minidress hugged her curves. The top was cut out to expose her full breasts and hard nipples. She stepped close to speak in my ear. "Let's dance, honey."

I shook my head. "No, thanks. I don't dance."

She laughed, tossing her long black hair over her shoulder. "What do you mean you don't dance? Everyone dances."

She grabbed my hand, and half-pulled, half-dragged me back

to the dance area. She walked over to the corner of the room, right next to the speakers. The bass sent vibrations through my body.

She held me close, her arm around my waist, her crotch grinding against the dildo. Her black hair swayed with the music, her hips gyrating. A small group cheered us on. If Matt could only see me now.

I played along, enjoying the music. Until she cupped my breast with one hand. I jumped back and fast-walked away from her.

She followed me to the bar. "I knew it. Just another straight girl playing it up for the straight men. Typical."

"Fuck off," I shouted back.

She laughed. "Tease. Go home, little girl. These grown-up games aren't for the merely vanilla." She dismissed me with a flip of her hair. Turned around to walk away.

What I did next, well, I don't know how it happened, but I think that her calling me "vanilla" was the final straw. Her words flipped a switch in me. I was fed up with people assuming that I lacked flavor, that I wasn't kinky enough. First Matt and now a complete stranger.

That's why I grabbed her shoulder, turned her around, and gave her the best kiss of my life. I put passion and fire into that kiss. It must have been good because she went so limp that I could have poured her into a water bucket.

The music, the cheering crowd, the kiss . . . it all made me dizzy. I swayed on my feet, holding onto the bar for support. It was a good thing. When she dropped to her knees, I couldn't believe what I was seeing.

She smiled up at me while she played with the dildo. Teasing it with her tongue. Licking the hard shaft, sliding up and down.

Cameras flashed when she took the tip into her mouth. She moaned, eyes closed, her mouth working my fake cock.

The pressure of her mouth pushed the harness against me. Pressing the front against my clit, rubbing gently. The sensations were nice, but watching her was something else. The way she played with my cock, sneaking glances to see my reaction. Searching my face for signs of approval.

It was a complete power trip. Now I understood why guys loved to watch women suck their cocks. She worshipped my dildo, making me wet. Making me want to do naughty things to her. When I couldn't take it anymore, I grabbed her by the hand and took her to the closest bathroom.

We had a small audience, but neither of us cared. I couldn't wait to try the harness for the first time, for real. I placed her in front of one of the sinks. Bent her over so that her hands were on the cold porcelain. Kicked her legs apart and tilted her ass toward me.

I watched her face in the mirror while I adjusted the harness. Positioned the base of the cock right over my clit. Still looking at her, I pushed her dress up, caressing her firm ass. As I expected, she wasn't wearing anything underneath. The dildo slid into her easily.

My first few strokes were tentative. I couldn't tell how deep I was going, and I didn't want to hurt her. With a few grunts, she urged me on. Wanting more of it. Wanting it deeper.

Grabbing her by the hips, I fucked her with long strokes. Taking my time. I studied her reflection, the way her pretty face became serious, focused on her orgasm. Her bare breasts bounced with each thrust. Her hand slipped between her legs, rubbing at her exposed clit.

The base of the dildo pressed against me. I wanted to touch

myself, but I didn't. I wanted her to come. I wanted to make her come. I thrust faster, harder until she was moaning, grunting, making so much noise that more people poked their heads around the door until we had our own small crowd.

It was the first time I ever saw a woman come in person and not on film. Her brows curled into a frown, and her bottom lip pushed out in an exaggerated pout. After a deep thrust, she arched her spine, threw her head back. Her face clenched and then relaxed, a giggle bubbling out of her lips. I'm not lying when I say she glowed.

She wasn't at all thankful, the little bitch. Not a kiss, a good-bye, or even a smile back before she was out the door and off to wiggle her pussy in someone else's face. Using warm water, I washed her juice off the dildo. I looked up at myself in the mirror. It was a little bizarre to see my dark nipples and definitely womanly body with a realistic cock, particularly one that I was currently stroking.

I readjusted the buckles and snaps, making sure it all fit right and tight. I made one more change before I went back out. I tossed my blouse into the trash can. I'd blend into the crowd better topless.

I hadn't been in the bathroom for very long. Still, the action in the rest of the place had intensified. Ice cubes were being thrown around. People were piggy-backing each other. The hired go-go dancers were screaming. People were fucking every-where. On barstools. Against the walls. On the dance floor— some standing, some on their knees, and some on their backs.

I suddenly realized why my ex-boyfriend found this event, this place, so alluring. I could be anything I wanted. I could do anything I wanted. And no matter how bizarre I thought my own fantasies were, someone else's fantasies were even further out there.

I started dancing. My hands up. My hips and ass shaking. My breasts flashing and rolling in time to the beat. One guy fastened his mouth on one of my breasts and another pressed his cock against the crack of my ass. And at that exact moment my eyes fastened on Matt's. I stopped dead. Since I wasn't moving any longer, the strangers lost interest and moved off, but Matt moved in.

He looked duller than I remembered. His black slacks were tight, his button-up shirt was spread open, and he'd painted half his face purple. But that was it. About as unusual and erotic as you'd find in the bleachers of a football game.

"Hey," was as much as he could say as his eyes fluttered between my real tits and my fake cock.

"Who's vanilla now?" I laughed.

"You look incredible. Can't believe it." He cooed and in case his kiss-and-make-up attitude wasn't clear enough, he said, "What the hell was I thinking?"

Matt had hurt me. I didn't expect the breakup. Never thought I'd be dumped because I wasn't exciting enough. But maybe he was right. I sure did like the new me. All the eroticism. All the power. And, perhaps, a whole lot more satisfying sex.

Had I come here to make him jealous, to show him what he was missing, or hoping to win him back? It was time to be honest. I was here for a revenge fuck and a final good-bye, my way and my terms. I wanted to be this new wild, hot, erotic woman for myself and not in spite of him. But if spite was how I met this new me, then so be it.

I grabbed Matt by the hand and took him to the closest bathroom.

Just as I had with the girl, I placed him in front of one of the sinks. Bent him over so that his hands were on the cold porcelain. Kicked his legs apart and tilted his ass toward me.

"Matt," I murmured in his ear as I slid the dildo into his straining ass, "what flavor am I now?"

Neil Truitt

JennaTip #13: Getting Behind Sex—for Him

One main difference between vaginal sex and anal sex has to do with the fact that your ass is not meant to have anything pushed into it. It was created as an exit only. That doesn't mean you cannot break the rules. It just means that things need to be handled a little differently.

The anus will suck in when pressed against. Not so much with the vagina. If you are playing around there with a finger, don't be freaked out if you feel like your finger is being pulled into his ass. That's exactly what's happening.

Going back to Tip #2, LUBE, LUBE, LUBE! Also, relax! DO NOT CLENCH!

Once the finger or butt plug or other item (clean item, please) is inside an inch or so, point it toward the taint (slang for the area between his balls and his asshole), and rub or push there. That's his prostate. He can come just from this. But why not go ahead and play with his cock and balls to make it that much more amazing? He'll thank you.

If he isn't ready for penetration, then you can push on the taint and stroke it and he'll get something like the same feeling, but the orgasm and ejaculation won't be as powerful.

Guys! Wash yourself down there. It's for your health and also for her pleasure.

About Sounds Publishing, Inc.

Sounds Publishing Inc. was founded in 2004 by the husband-and-wife team of Brian and Catherine OliverSmith, with the goal of bringing high-quality romantic and erotic content to life in a variety of mediums. As the leading provider of romance and erotica in audio, their company produces healthy, sexy erotica, encouraging people to increase romance, intimacy, and passion through fantasy.

About the Editor

M. Catherine OliverSmith is the cofounder and editor-in-chief of Sounds Publishing, a co-venture with her spouse, Brian OliverSmith. She is the editor of hundreds of short stories and more than nine compilations and anthologies. She served as editor-in-chief of *The Docket*, the official newspaper of the UCLA School of Law, and is the mother of two beautiful girls.

She would like to thank her husband, partner, lover, and best friend, Brian, for making good on his promise that life would never be boring.

About the Cover Photographer

Photographer Mike Ruiz is best known for his high-impact, colorful celebrity and fashion photography. His artistic objective is to present an upscale fashion edge to sensuality with aspirational images of iconic personas. Of all the celebrities he has photographed—from Kirsten Dunst to Ricky Martin to Christina Aguilera, just to name a few—he says he can count on one hand those that he believes truly possess the special unique magic to light up a camera. Jenna Jameson is one.

A mutual friend introduced Ruiz to Jameson for a spec shoot that turned out to be so successful, Jameson asked Ruiz to create the images for her new series of erotica, JennaTales. "Jenna has this amazing chemistry with the lens," explains Ruiz. "She loves the camera and the camera reciprocates that love. Every shot is beautiful."

Though a majority of his work has been with major magazines like *Vanity Fair* and *Interview* in the U.S., and European publications such as *Italian Elle*, *Arena*, and *Dazed and Confused*, Mike Ruiz has contributed to several books including Dolce and Gabbana's *Hollywood* and Iman's *The Beauty of Color*.

In addition to his editorial assignments, Ruiz has shot advertising campaigns for Sean John, MAC Cosmetics, and Reebok. He worked alongside rapper Lil Kim to create the image for her Royalty watch line and has recently branched out as a director, creating music videos for Traci Lords and Kelly Rowland.

This fall, Mike Ruiz made his feature film directorial debut with *Starrbooty*, a new madcap spy/comedy adventure starring the original supermodel of the world, RuPaul. For more information on Mike Ruiz and his projects, visit his website atwww.mikeruiz.com.

PUT DOWN THE BOOK . . . and experience hot, sexy erotica in a whole new hands-free way!

Sounds Publishing offers a wide variety of short audio erotica via download at www.jennatales.com and other online retailers.

Visit www.jennatales.com for a FREE erotic tale from the Sounds Publishing collection today.

Browse the several titles available for hands-free enjoyment on your MP3 player, iPod, burned to a CD, or directly on your computer.

Other titles from Sounds Publishing, Inc.

In print:

JennaTales: Erotica for the Woman on Top
   Something Borrowed (May 2008)
   Lip Service (July 2008)
   Happy Endings (September 2008)

In audio:

Dulce Amore	*Tongue & Tied*
Melt Away	*A Lick & a Promise*
Kiss Your Ear	*Bend, Lick, Insert, Send*
Nibbles & Bites	*You've Got Tail*

Share Your Fantasies—Be a JennaTales Contributor!

Why not share your favorite, hottest, and best fantasy with the world? Send Sounds Publishing your short, erotic tale for **Jenna-Tales,** *Erotica for the Woman on Top,* and if it is chosen to be developed into an audio story or included in a future **JennaTales** collection of erotica, receive a **free CD.**

Visit www.jennatales.com for submission guidelines and official rules.

Ask Jenna About . . .

In developing **JennaTips,** *Sex Tips for the Woman on Top,* we want to answer *your* burning questions. Tell us exactly what it is you want. Maybe one of the stories really lit your fire and you want more details about how to act it out. Maybe you're just curious about something you've heard about, read about, seen performed, or imagined.

Visit www.jennatales.com and click on the Ask Jenna! link to e-mail us your question. Keep your eyes out for the upcoming **JennaTips,** *Sex Tips for the Woman on Top* books.

Become the woman on top.

*A few choice tidbits and excerpts from **Something Borrowed**, the second in the hugely popular **JennaTales** series of sexy anthologies. Whatever your fancy, these inventive and entertaining, wickedly wanton stories will delight you.*

Girl Gone Wild

I'm really more reserved than this story sets me up to be, but once I've had a few drinks—and by a few, I mean 4-plus—I have this thing about being naked. Well, maybe not naked as in stripper naked, but naked as in peep show.

Winner Takes Half

At six feet, one-half inch in my bare feet, I'm a tall, lithe force to be reckoned with and, except for my rather impressive breasts, I'm tri-athlete thin with long legs that do go all the way up, toned arms, and a mane of red hair I streak with gold for even greater impact. I'm called "Tigress."

Getting Her Move On

I placed two boxes on the bedroom floor, then unbuttoned my shirt and took it off. I wasn't trying to show off, though the weekend moving jobs kept my muscles toned. I was just hot and figured that my arms were a better sight than sweat soaking through my clothes.

*Toss out your corny confessional collections that once upon a time tickled your fantasy and replace them with all the **JennaTales**, erotica for the woman on top titles to liberate your libido. **Something Borrowed** is coming to a bookstore near you—May 2008.*